# The Glass Forest

*A Cara Walden Mystery*

# Books by Lisa Lieberman

## Cara Walden Mysteries

*The Glass Forest*

*Burning Cold*

*All the Wrong Places*

## History

*Apologizing for Vietnam*

*Stalin's Boots: In the Footsteps of the Failed 1956 Hungarian Revolution*

*Dirty War: Terror and Torture in French Algeria*

*Leaving You: The Cultural Meaning of Suicide*

## Translations

Simone de Beauvoir, *An Eye for an Eye*

Jean-Paul Sartre, *Paris Under the Occupation*

# The Glass Forest

## Lisa Lieberman

Passport Press

The epigraph comes from Hieu Minh Nguyen, *Not Here* (Coffee House Press, 2018). Graham Greene references are from the 2004 Penguin edition of *The Quiet American* unless otherwise noted. The line from "The Tale of Kiêu" comes from the *Yale Review* translation published in a bilingual edition in 1983 by Yale University Press.

Book design and conversion by Eddie Vincent/Encircle Publications
Cover design by Deirdre Wait/Encircle Publications
Passport Press logo design by Timothy Lang
Author Photo by Sharona Jacobs

## Publisher's Cataloging-in-Publication data

Names: Lieberman, Lisa, author.
Title: The Glass forest / Lisa Lieberman.
Series: A Cara Walden Mystery
Description: Amherst, MA: Passport Press, 2019.
Identifiers: LCCN 2019911002 | ISBN 978-0-9989837-3-8 (pbk.) | 978-0-9989837-4-5 (ebook)
Subjects: LCSH Greene, Graham, 1904-1991. The Quiet American--Fiction. | Ho Chi Minh City (Vietnam)--History--Fiction. | Vietnam (Republic)--History--20th century--Fiction. | Vietnam--History--1945-1975--Fiction. | Families--Fiction. | Brothers and sisters - Fiction. | Gay men--Fiction. | Mystery and detective stories. | Suspense fiction. | BISAC FICTION / Mystery & Detective / Historical | FICTION /Mystery & Detective / International Crime | FICTION / Noir
Classification: LCC PS3612.I3347 G53 2019 | DDC 813.6--dc23

*For Ben, Carey, and Hannah*

# CHAPTER ONE

## Continental Palace Hotel, Saigon
## March 9, 1957

*Let me be clear: any love I find will be treason.*
Hieu Minh Nguyen

Although it was not yet dark, the restaurant staff were setting the tables for dinner, laying white cloths, cutlery, wineglasses, crystal vases with sprigs of frangipani—and still Tam hadn't come. Jakub and I were having an apéritif on the terrace with my brother Gray and ordinarily this would have been our signal to finish up. The Continental's French cuisine was so heavy, cream sauces and braised meats unpalatable in the humid climate. We much preferred the Chinese food at the Rainbow. Tam considered the Rainbow a tourist trap, overpriced and too westernized for his liking, but that didn't prevent him from patronizing the upstairs nightclub, where cool jazz could be heard any night of the week.

"I think I'll head over now, if the two of you don't mind," said Gray. "He's probably in the bar, hounding Murphy for an autograph." His lover's disapproval of Western cultural influences did not extend to movie Westerns either. They'd met in the air-conditioned Majestic Cinema at a late matinee of *The Cimarron Kid,* where my brother (no fan of Audie Murphy) had gone to escape the heat. Tam was watching the picture for the second time, and might have stayed for the seven o'clock showing had the usher not insisted he purchase a new ticket.

Jakub shook his head. "Murphy's gone. Mankiewicz gave him permission to leave after they ran the rushes of the disaster scene. Most of the stars cleared out on Thursday."

"Before the wrap party?" My brother stroked his chin, a lingering habit from when he wore a goatee.

"That was just for the crew."

Too late I perceived the flaw in the story I'd concocted to cover his absence. Tam couldn't have been chaperoning the cast around Saigon's lesser-known shopping districts if they were already en route to Rome. But Gray had no reason to suspect that I knew more than he did regarding his lover's whereabouts. So successfully had he distanced himself from the production of *The Quiet American* that he'd lost track of the actors' comings and goings.

My husband was more astute. In the short time we'd been sitting outside, I'd smoked four cigarettes, my vermouth cassis untouched on the table between us. Of course he'd noticed. The pedicab bearing Gray to the Rainbow had barely pulled away from the curb when Jakub reached for my hand.

"*Najdroższa,*" he said, employing the Polish endearment he always used in place of my name. "What's going on?" I saw the concern in his dark brown eyes and wondered how long I could keep the truth from him. I didn't used to be good at lying and a part of me wanted to be caught.

"Let's take a walk," I suggested.

Jakub signed for our drinks and we were soon ambling along rue Catinat, the graceful French boulevard that nobody called by its new Vietnamese name, heading away from the river toward Paris Square and the red towers of Notre-Dame. It had rained earlier in the afternoon, a sudden shower that left the air blurry with vapor, tiny prisms glinting in the sun-pierced mist. Such sights had delighted me when we arrived. Everything about Saigon felt new and exotic: live crabs being sold out of bowls filled with water, right on the sidewalk. Tiny shrines the size of dollhouses in unexpected places throughout the city. There was one in front of the bank a few steps from our hotel and customers would pause and bow before entering, to safeguard themselves against the malice of wandering souls. The mounds of dragon fruit in the market, with their green scales and leathery pink skin. Slice one in half and inside you'd find translucent white flesh polka-dotted with black seeds. I'd expected them to taste tangy, like pineapple, but the fruit was nearly flavorless, with a mushy feel in the mouth. Nothing here was what it seemed.

In two days we'd be on an Air France jet to Rome. They'd be shooting the interior scenes at Cinecittà, but thankfully our involvement with *The Quiet American* would be over. I say "our involvement," but only Jakub was still tied to the production, although Gray continued to draw a salary from Figaro. He'd been brought in to doctor the script, but there was no saving it.

*Mankiewicz won't hear of changing a single word*, Gray had written to us in Paris. *He's making a piece of lousy propaganda, a travesty of the Graham Greene novel. I was just hired as window dressing. Fascinating place, Saigon.* He'd begged us to come out and keep him company, luring us with the promise of jobs on the set of *The Quiet American*. Jakub, who was fluent in four languages, was put to work immediately translating for the Polish, French, and Italian members of the crew. Sadly, I was fired on my first day as an extra, after getting on the wrong side of the local fixer.

Jakub said: "Tam's made up his mind. He's joined the insurgency, hasn't he?" No point in asking how he knew. My husband had served as a courier in the French underground during the war. A music student at the Paris Conservatoire whose family back in Poland had been consigned to the Warsaw Ghetto, he'd had no choice but to take up with the Communist Resistance after the French police began rounding up foreign-born Jews and deporting them. He had been twenty years old, friendless, and the Party gave him a purpose, as well as a sense of belonging.

"They left him no choice," I confirmed. There would be no turning back for him now.

We'd reached our destination, a tree-lined square with the Catholic church smack in the center. As we waited to cross the street, a man wearing a conical bamboo hat pedaled by on a bicycle laden with vegetables from the market. But for him, and the cluster of schoolgirls in white *ao dais* gossiping on the corner, we might have been on any broad boulevard in Paris at the end of the working day. I so longed to be back there.

"Ready, Cara? Let's go!" Jakub took my arm and together we plunged into the traffic. There are very few stoplights in Saigon, no lanes, no rules of the road that I could discern other than *sauve qui peut*: every man for himself. The trick to getting across an intersection is to keep moving in a straight line and at a steady pace. Miraculously, the cars and scooters would calculate your trajectory and steer around you.

A man was dead because of me, his body left not a mile from where we were standing. I'd expected the story to be front-page news, the murder of an American businessman in Saigon's tourist district, but the crime was being hushed up. If I told Jakub how I learned about Tam's decision to cast his lot with the Communists, I'd end up confessing the part I'd played in the American's murder. The desire to unburden myself of the terrible secret I'd been carrying around was so strong, but would it help? My husband might absolve me, but I would never forgive myself for setting the train of events in motion.

When we left Vietnam, I'd be leaving something important behind. My innocence.

# CHAPTER TWO

## Tây Ninh, Vietnam
## February 9, 1957

"Ladies, please. You too much in frame." Mr. Quang indicated a bubblegum pink pillar festooned with writhing plaster dragons and bade us stand behind it—myself, the script girl, and the production manager's secretary. You can't tell the pillar is bubblegum pink since the picture was filmed in black and white—a good thing because the interior of the Cao Dai Temple was far more distracting than we were, "a Walt Disney fantasia of the East, dragons and snakes in Technicolor," in the words of Graham Greene. Michael Redgrave recites Greene's description in a voiceover, omitting the Technicolor bit, as his journalist character, Fowler, enters the nave. He walks right by our pillar, but the take they used of the temple scene was shot from a high angle and from such a distance that you can't see us.

Honestly, I don't mind. The day was a disaster from start to finish, although Michael was charming, making small talk with us "ladies" between takes. He'd only recently arrived in Vietnam and was having a dreadful time adjusting to the humidity. I'd had a week to get used to it and wasn't faring much better. Inside the temple it was ten degrees cooler and I remember him joking about muffing the scene on purpose, to have an excuse to stay out of the sun.

Mankiewicz generally avoided filming at midday because the strong light made everything flat. You notice it in the religious procession, the opening sequence that establishes Fowler's presence in Tây Ninh, the Rome of the Cao Dai faith. The cardinals look washed out in their white robes as they march through the streets of the town, but it's a key event in the novel, the annual pageant in the Cao Dai Holy See. Filming it on location, as opposed to staging it at Cinecittà, gave the picture an authentic, travelogue feel. That and Michael's performance are the best that can be said for it, if you want my opinion.

The Cao Dai pageant had been going on since the religion was founded, back in the 1920s, but the French didn't bother attending until the Cao Dai pope recruited his own militia after World War II, when the Communists began massacring his adherents. The colonial authorities wanted to be sure the private army would not be used against them, and so began courting the movement's leaders. It was time-consuming, not to mention risky, driving out from Saigon through territory controlled by the Việt Minh. Members of the Diplomatic Corps, according to Greene, "would send a few second secretaries with their wives and girls" instead of making the journey themselves.

That's who we were supposed to be, but I didn't look matronly enough to be convincing as a diplomat's wife. With my pixie cut, and wearing only a trace of lipstick, I appeared a good deal younger than my twenty-three years, more like someone's girlfriend (although Greene used the word "girl" as shorthand for Vietnamese mistress). Both the script girl and the production manager's secretary, I observed, were wearing blouses buttoned all the way up, and tailored skirts. Work clothes. In comparison, I looked as if I were heading off to the beach in my sleeveless shift and low-heeled sandals. What was I thinking?

"Too much shoulders." Mr. Quang snapped his fingers to summon the wardrobe mistress, and all work stopped until she was found. I wanted to disappear, I was so embarrassed. At least Jakub was up with the technical crew in the balcony, setting up lights, running sound checks and whatnot. The sanctuary was quite vast and I doubted he was aware of what was going on in our corner down below.

"He treats everyone like that," said the wardrobe mistress consolingly, draping a shawl around my shoulders. "Don't let it bother you, hon. It'll soon be forgotten."

I wished I could believe her. Mr. Quang struck me as the meticulous sort who never forgot anything, not that I blamed him. The honorific "mister" notwithstanding, he was little more than a glorified dogsbody on the production, albeit one with privileges. Rumor had it that he auditioned "girls" (in Greene's sense) to keep Mankiewicz company in his hotel room at night, and his standards were said to be very exacting. Growing up in Hollywood, I knew all about the shenanigans that went on behind the scenes, starlets exchanging sexual favors in exchange for a role. Auditions on the casting couch. Men set the price of admission and women paid, each one hoping that she'd be the exception: the one who made it and became a star, finding true love along the way. It bothered me because my own mother, Vivien, had been one of those exceptions, and it hadn't made her happy at all.

Mankiewicz's girls, like Fowler's Vietnamese mistress in *The Quiet American*, were easily disposed of, once they'd served their purpose. I was afraid that Mr. Quang put me in the same category and I thought it prudent to stay out of his way from that point onwards. When they finished the scene, I lingered in the temple instead of following the others outdoors. Since childhood, I was accustomed to entertaining myself on the set of whichever picture Father happened to be directing. Nobody paid attention as I poked around, inventing magical adventures for myself among the props and scenery, so long as I kept away from where they were actually filming. The set in this case was certainly magical. Whose idea was it to paint clouds on the sky blue ceiling? And what was the meaning of the giant globe with an eye painted on it that stood where the altar would be positioned in a Christian church? I'd have to read up on the religion when we were back in Saigon.

Worshipers were returning to the sanctuary to pray. I kept the shawl on, to avoid offending the devout with my bare shoulders. It was quite garish, the shawl, a floral pattern in pinks and oranges that matched the inside of the temple. I guess the Cao Dai liked bright colors. A pair of elderly monks in yellow robes nodded approvingly in my direction as they made their way to the altar.

". . . *les bannières. Les avez-vous vu?*" I caught a snippet of their whispered conversation: the banners. Did you see them?

It surprised me, how many Vietnamese spoke French in public. They seemed content to continue using the language, even after they'd kicked the colonizers out. I'd been taught French in boarding school—enough to order from a menu in a posh restaurant, as my friends and I used to say, to make polite conversation with French people on social occasions, or to parse the labels beneath the paintings in the Louvre. It was that kind of boarding school. The two monks spoke the language far more colloquially than I did, and the rest

9

of their conversation was lost to me. I wasn't even sure I'd understood the bit I heard. Banners?

I found out later what they were talking about. We'd returned from Tây Ninh at the end of the afternoon and were unwinding in the rooftop bar of the Majestic Hotel. Most of the cast and crew were staying there, including Gray; Jakub and I were at the Continental because by the time we'd arrived they'd run out of room at the Majestic.

The bar overlooked the Saigon River and from its balcony you could watch the big ships navigating along it for miles. Small fishing vessels darted around them. As the sun went down, the fishermen hung lanterns in the bow and stern, to make themselves visible to the behemoths. It was mesmerizing, the lights of the little boats dancing like dragonflies above the surface of the water, flickering against the glow of the red-streaked horizon.

Jakub had come to stand beside me at the railing. "Some view," he said, slipping an arm around my shoulders and pulling me close. We fit so well, my head just level with his shoulder. We'd met by chance on a beach in Southern Italy, and I'd known instantly that he was the one.

"Wonderful! Are you glad we came, darling?" I was happy anywhere, so long as he was with me, but my husband had opted not to bring his violin on account of the humidity and I feared he missed playing music.

"Mmmm-hmmm," he murmured into my hair. Turning me to face him, he tipped my chin up and kissed me, softly, teasingly. A promise of more to come, and one that I intended to hold him to, as soon as we were alone. The Majestic's rooftop bar was hardly the place for intimacy. People had been drinking for several hours and the conversations around us were being conducted at high volume, with much slurring of words.

"Moses, Jesus, Buddha, Mohammed, Confucius. I believe the Virgin Mary's in there too." Bill Hornbeck, the film's editor, was ticking off the saints in the Cao Dai pantheon. Judging from his clear enunciation, he was not a drinker, which didn't surprise me. Of all the key personnel, I liked Bill best. He'd worked on some top pictures: *It's a Wonderful Life*, *Shane*, *A Place in the Sun,* and *Giant*. They did well, thanks to his editing expertise. He'd won Oscars for both *It's a Wonderful Life* and *A Place in the Sun,* but the awards hadn't gone to his head. He was a very decent guy who put in long days and went to bed early. And alone. Bill's wife was due to arrive the following week and he was so eager to see her you'd think they were newlyweds, like Jakub and me, instead of a settled couple.

"You've left out Shakespeare," someone said.

"Shakespeare?" My brother's voice rose above the fray. He also liked his liquor, but knew enough, thankfully, to limit his drinking while he was on a job. "Shakespeare's not a religious personage."

"Neither is Charlie Chaplin, and they revere him," Bill replied matter-of-factly.

This got Gray's attention. He viewed Charlie Chaplin as a genius of the same magnitude as Einstein. Indeed, Graham Greene's championing of Chaplin after the US government banned him as a Communist sympathizer in 1952 is what initially got my brother reading the British author. Gray himself had been blacklisted by that time and had fled to London to avoid naming names before HUAC, the House Committee on Un-American Activities, taking me along. Very few public figures were speaking out against McCarthy's witch hunt in America. Greene became his hero, which made it all the more galling, the way that Mankiewicz had butchered the novel for his screenplay of *The Quiet American*, turning it into an anti-Communist screed.

"It's a strange religion. The priests use a Ouija board to communicate with the spirits of their saints and heroes." If it were anyone else saying this, I'd have thought they were making it up, but Bill was dead earnest.

My brother was incredulous. "Charlie Chaplin sent them a message through a Ouija board? Why couldn't he just pick up the phone?" A waiter came by with a tray of fruity cocktails adorned with paper umbrellas, but Gray, intent on hearing the story, waved him away.

"No, it's only the dead who've had to resort to occult means of communication," Bill explained in his patient manner. Jakub and I moved closer, to learn more. The editor had done a fair amount of research on the Vietnamese sect. "There've been posthumous messages from Victor Hugo, Louis Pasteur, Napoleon Bonaparte, and Joan of Arc."

"Talkative bunch, the French," muttered Gray.

"Always," said my husband, laughing. "Just get one of them started on the subject of religion or philosophy and then try to get a word in edgewise."

I shushed them and asked Bill what the messages were about. The idea of communicating with the dead was so compelling. What if, when someone died, she wasn't really gone? What if you and she could have a conversation, from time to time? I'd lost Vivien when I was ten years old and there was so much I wanted to talk to her about, things that only a mother would understand. I'd settle for putting questions to her via a Ouija board if that's what it took to feel her presence in my life again. Sometimes I struggled to remember her, she'd died so long ago. I'd look through my collection of publicity stills from the pictures she'd starred in until I found one that spoke to me, a shot of Vivien where she'd allowed something of her true self, the person I remembered, to come through.

"The only message I'm aware of was from Joan of Arc," the editor was saying, "but it was very inspiring. Just a minute, I have it written down somewhere." He fumbled in his jacket pocket, extracting a pamphlet, one of many I'd noticed in the temple's vestibule. There were stacks of them, translated into various languages for tourists, but I hadn't thought to pick one up.

"Here we go." Bill's eyes scanned the page. "Let's see. She told them to keep up the good fight against the French. 'I was a soldier in a liberation army, just as you are, seeking your freedom from the occupying French. Your struggle was my struggle—' "

"Hold on," said Gray. "That's radical stuff. You're not telling us they worship revolutionaries in that church."

"That's precisely what I'm telling you. Sun Yat-sen is a Cao Dai saint, and so is Vladimir Lenin."

My brother let out a whistle of appreciation. "Lenin too? I'm surprised they can get away with it. Bolshevism predicted the fall of colonial regimes. My God, Lenin couldn't wait to see the whole imperialist structure come crashing down. Did his damnedest to help make it happen. The French couldn't have turned a blind eye to the Cao Dai if they were venerating him."

"Oh, they've had their share of run-ins with the authorities," agreed Bill. "The French used to lock up their leaders, from time to time, and the current Vietnamese government recently forced their pope into exile. That's what yesterday's protest demonstration was about."

"Protest demonstration? What protest demonstration?" Jakub wanted to know. Of the three of us, he was the only one who'd been in Tây Ninh for the filming of the procession

13

the previous day. Gray and I had stayed in Saigon and visited the zoo, where I'd encountered my first water buffalo. First and second: a breeding pair. They were awfully cute.

Bill slid the pamphlet back into his pocket and helped himself to a canapé from a nearby table of hors d'oeuvres.

"It didn't look like a protest demonstration," he said between bites of pâté. He picked up the plate and proffered it around. "You ought to try one of these, it's the best thing they do here." I took one to be polite, but he was right. I wasn't fond of chopped liver, but the Majestic's pâté had a chiffon-like texture and was seasoned with ginger, a perfect melding of French and Asian cuisines.

"Delicious," I said, taking another canapé. The Majestic's cocktails were rather strong and I was feeling lightheaded. Getting some food in my stomach was a good idea.

Bill returned to his story. "Some of the marchers were carrying banners demanding the return of the pope. We didn't know what they said—it was all in Vietnamese—but they caused a ruckus among the onlookers. Later we learned the truth. Fortunately, the police thought we'd staged the scene for the film and didn't intervene. We captured the entire thing and it's brilliant."

"You show them footage?" Mr. Quang had come out of nowhere to insert himself into the conversation.

"No."

"You show them footage." This time it was not phrased as a question.

I have an expressive face, an asset for an actress, less so for a singer. You don't want the audience looking at your face for cues to how they should respond to the music, you want the song to hit them right in the gut. In the Paris nightclubs where I perform with Jakub's trio, I've learned to channel my emotions into my voice, keeping my expression neutral. If only I'd thought to mask my reaction to Mr. Quang's pronouncement. Disapproval at the peremptory tone he'd used with Bill must have been plain for all to see.

"Girl in temple," he said.

I'd changed into evening clothes, an off-the-shoulder cocktail dress from Italy and stiletto heels that added inches to my height, but he still recognized me, and those three words sealed my fate. Mr. Quang hadn't hired me, but he had the power to get me fired. The next morning, while Jakub and I were having breakfast in the inner courtyard of our hotel, the bellhop delivered an envelope with my name handwritten on it. Inside was a typed memorandum on the Figaro letterhead signed by Mankiewicz himself informing me that I was no longer needed as an extra. Wordlessly, I passed the missive across the table.

"I'm sorry, *najdroższa*." Gentleman that he was, my husband offered to resign that very day, but it wouldn't have been fair, making him give up a job he enjoyed, particularly since we had come to Vietnam at my urging. He'd befriended a number of Polish crew members and it wasn't often that he got to speak his native tongue on a regular basis. Also, he was paid well for his services, earning more in a day than the trio earned in a week on tour. We'd be in good shape when we got back to Paris.

It didn't matter immediately, my being out of work. The entire production was shut down for a week because one of the stars was ailing. Audie Murphy had hopped over to Hong Kong to do a little sightseeing and had come down with a bug. His health was fragile, what with all his war injuries, and the heat seemed to affect him more than it affected others. While he recuperated in the hospital over there, the rest of us were free to do as we pleased.

Gray was eager to get out of the city. He'd arrived with

the advance team to scout locations in early January and had already been in Saigon for a month before Jakub and I joined him. He'd been lonely, I could tell. In London, he moved in artistic circles, but the English-speaking community here was largely comprised of businessmen and American military personnel, not the kind of company he found congenial. My brother was left to his own devices. Faced with a similar situation in the past, he'd have taken refuge in drink, and I'd been afraid he'd lapse back into it if we didn't come. He'd looked out for me, when I was younger, doing his best to compensate for Vivien's absence. Now that I was an adult, I tried to do the same for him.

The three of us debated how to spend our impromptu vacation. Some of the cast were off to the beach. The closest resort, Vũng Tàu, was a scant two-hour drive away. Others chose to do a bit of historical sightseeing, flying out to visit the ruins of the temple complex of Angkor Wat in Cambodia. We settled on a combination of the two, beginning with a tour of the Imperial City in Huế, a short flight from Saigon, followed by a few days at a former French resort on the central coast. Gray was toying with the idea of writing a novel set in Vietnam, like Greene's, and wanted to see more of the country. I think he'd have liked to visit Hanoi and get the North Vietnamese perspective on the war—Hồ Chí Minh intrigued him—but of course this was out of the question.

Huế was the closest we could get. The seat of the Nguyễn dynasty, it spoke of Vietnam's long history of conquest and endurance. To put it in the words of Pascal, our Vietnamese guide: *Trong khi ngô-biên tông quyën biët sao.* When evil strikes, you bow to circumstance.

# CHAPTER THREE

## The Imperial City
## February 10, 1957

A steady drizzle and not another soul in sight. I tried to imagine the Imperial City as a vibrant place, as opposed to the empty mausoleum it had become. Pascal was explaining how the first Nguyễn emperor, Gia Long, had consulted a geomancer, an astrologer trained in divination, to find the best location for his royal complex.

"Win?" said Gray. "Is that how you pronounce N–g–u–y–e–n?"

"Yes. In the north, however, we have the rising tone. The voice, she goes up like a question."

A small man with a scholarly air, our guide had taught literature in a prestigious Hanoi lycée for some thirty years, abandoning both home and career in the wake of the Việt Minh victory over the French to join the hundreds of thousands of North Vietnamese Catholics fleeing Communist persecution. I'd seen a newsreel about the exodus, when Gray and I were living in London. The American Navy sent ships to the port in Haiphong as part of a rescue operation, Passage to Freedom, but the number of terrified migrants kept increasing. There were stories of appalling crimes against Catholics: priests castrated, women violated, old men tortured, Communist soldiers sticking chopsticks in schoolchildren's ears when they caught them praying. My brother had warned me that these stories should be taken with a grain of salt. Atrocities were committed by both sides in times of war, violence exaggerated for propaganda purposes, he said, but I'd been horrified regardless. People wouldn't be risking their lives to get out of North Vietnam for no good reason. Was the fact that both sides were terrorizing the population supposed to make it okay?

I studied Pascal as he talked. He did not look like someone who'd been brutalized—not that I knew what to look for. His eyes were tired, behind his wire-rimmed spectacles, but he carried himself with dignity. He'd had no success in finding a new teaching position since coming to Hué, he admitted, and was supporting himself with various odd jobs, from translating to private tutoring. We were his first tourists, and he clearly relished having a captive audience once again.

"Traditionally, Vietnamese, like Chinese, look to celestial creatures for protection." This site on the north bank of the Perfume River, overlooking Ngu Binh Mountain, was considered auspicious because of the two sand dunes on the opposite bank of the Perfume River. "Dragon on the left, tiger on the right," he said, describing the shapes with an elegant, flowing motion of his hands.

They might have paid a little more attention to the weather, I thought sourly. Huddled beneath umbrellas, we could barely see the mountain through the fog rising off the river, let alone discern more subtle features of the landscape. We'd been trooping around the outside of the fortress for half an hour already while our guide drew our attention to various architectural elements. At this rate, we'd be soaking wet by the end of the afternoon, when we boarded our train for the coast. At least we'd have sunshine on the other end. Da Nang had a rainy season, but it was in the fall, not year-round as in Huế.

"Gia Long, he constructed the Citadels across Vietnam, all of them in the style of Vauban. You know who was Vauban?" Our guide crossed his arms and waited, as if trying to coax a response from recalcitrant pupils. "You do not know? French children, they know, and my students, I teach them this. Vauban was the engineer of Louis Quatorze, *le roi soleil*."

"The Sun King," said Jakub, duly chastened. "Was this supposed to be Gia Long's Versailles?"

"Not exactly. The fortress, she is French. The walls, if you are interested, are ten kilometers long and two meters thick, but the inside is not at all French. Now, if you will follow me, please, I will show you the Imperial City."

He led us through an archway and we emerged into an entirely new realm. Here, everything looked Chinese: temples and palaces with tiled, pagoda-style roofs, their corners guarded by snarling beasts with long tongues and spiky tails. Ornamental gardens, ponds filled with lotus flowers, and colorfully painted wooden gates, all converging on the Purple Forbidden City, an inner sanctum modeled on the Forbidden City in Peking. Members of the Nguyễn dynasty ruled French Indochina from this very spot, we learned, beginning in 1802 right up though the end of World War II, when the last of them, Emperor Bảo Đại, abdicated in favor of Hồ Chí Minh.

"Are you kidding me?" said Gray. "The Vietnamese emperor gave the Communists his blessing?"

Our guide frowned and promptly set the record straight. The emperor had been a puppet of Vichy and the Japanese.

The Việt Minh found him useful, as a figurehead, but when the French returned, he promptly changed sides.

"In other words," my brother said, "Bảo Đại sold himself to the highest bidder."

"Sold himself to the highest bidder." Pascal repeated the phrase with approval, adding it to his store of American colloquialisms. "Yes, and after the French defeat and the partition, he managed to get himself crowned head of state in the South, even though he was living in Paris. He appointed Ngo Dinh Diem to govern in his place."

Jakub laughed. "And Diem turned around and deposed him! Some gratitude."

"Two peas in a pod. That is the expression, no?" Our guide didn't wait for confirmation. "He is also a descendant of the Nguyễn, President Diem. Now, if you will come this way, I wish to show you the royal theater."

So, this was where all the tourists were, and no wonder, I thought as we entered the building. The theater was magnificent: red-lacquered walls, golden lanterns suspended from the ceiling, poetry written in Chinese script adorning the stage. Although much smaller than the Cao Dai Temple, the space felt sumptuous, befitting an emperor. Pascal took his time, showing us every last feature, but I didn't mind. It was dry inside the theater, and we were able to sit as we listened to our guide's account.

"Americans!" A pale blond man detached himself from a group of Vietnamese tourists and came toward us. "You have no idea what a relief it is, to run into some of my fellow countrymen in this godforsaken place. Mind if I join you?"

"This is a private tour," said Pascal, who had taken an instant dislike to the interloper. Cutting his lecture short, he ushered us out of the theater and bade us to follow him across a stone courtyard festooned with gigantic urns. He set a brisk pace, but our compatriot trotted right along beside us like a fawning golden retriever.

"Oh, come now. One more isn't going to hurt," he wheedled. "Tell him I'll pay double the going rate."

Our guide's reaction to this offer was a noncommittal shrug. The extra money might be welcome, but he left the decision on whether to include this ill-mannered stranger to us.

"Thanks!" The man already had his wallet out. "How much does he charge?"

"Eight hundred piastres," said Pascal curtly. I didn't blame him for being miffed. He was a good deal older than the rest of us, the blond fellow included, and was owed the courtesy of a direct address.

Our compatriot did a rapid calculation in his head and pulled five ten-dollar bills from his wallet. "Here you go, pal. Bet you'd rather have American money, eh?"

Pascal took the money, an expression of distaste on his face. We should have told the interloper to get lost. Not only was he crass, but now that he'd joined the tour, and paid double for the privilege, he couldn't stop chattering. Who were we? What brought us to Vietnam? How long had we been in the country?

"We're here for a tour," my husband said, silencing him for the time being.

The American fellow mimed zipping his lips shut. "Oops."

We'd arrived at the innermost structure of the Purple Forbidden City, a two-story pavilion perched atop a steep stone staircase. To reach it, you walked across a wide bridge spanning a murky pool. The pavilion's upper floor was shuttered, with a single fan-shaped opening cut into the painted wooden walls.

"Who lived here?" I asked. I couldn't imagine why anyone would have chosen to shut himself in a dark and airless building, so far from the main action of the palace.

"Trinh Minh palace was the residence of the royal concubines," our guide explained.

"Concubines!" Our compatriot could remain silent no longer. "Do you mean to tell us these emperors kept their girlfriends on the premises, right under the nose of their wives?"

Pascal ignored him. "The emperors—" He paused and turned to my husband, as if seeking permission to proceed with such a risqué subject in the presence of his wife. Or it may have been simply that he feared his English was not up to the task.

"*Ça va,*" said Jakub, switching to French. "*Ma femme n'est pas un enfant.*" My wife is not a child. I gave his hand a squeeze. One of the things I loved about him was that he didn't play games. Women pretending to be weak and incompetent, men afraid to show tenderness: he'd lost his entire family back in Poland, and yet he was in no way hardened by his experiences. Quite the opposite: he found life too precious to waste a single moment on trivialities.

But our guide's reticence had nothing to do with the prurience of the topic, as it turned out. "You must understand, it was an honor for a girl to be selected as the emperor's concubine. Only the daughters of mandarins were permitted to live in the interior city. They were groomed for the role, and their children were acknowledged as the emperor's heirs."

"Some honor," our compatriot interjected.

Privately, I couldn't help but agree. Concubines were just the royal counterpart to the girls Mr. Quang auditioned for Mankiewicz's pleasure. Prettied up with a fancy name and private accommodations, it was still exploitation. What became of those women when the emperor tired of them and their children? One early nineteenth-century ruler, Minh Mang, had three hundred wives and concubines and was supposed to have fathered a hundred and forty-two children over the course of twenty years, according to Pascal. Leaving aside the question of when he found time for governing his country, in and around all the hanky-panky, I couldn't help comparing him to the imperious monarch Yul Brynner played in *The King and I*. Deborah Kerr had her hands full, keeping him in line.

My friends and I used to complain, in boarding school, that our expensive education was turning us into luxury items, polished ornaments with no practical skills or serious interests, nothing that would get in the way of subsuming ourselves entirely beneath a husband's ambition. We were being groomed to become accessories to powerful men, but of course there was no comparison between the dreary marriages my friends and I contemplated, in our low moments, and the painted prison that was Trinh Minh palace. We had avenues of resistance unavailable to Vietnamese girls.

"Mandarins?" said Gray, steering the conversation to safer ground. "Do you mean there was an elite bureaucratic class here, just like in ancient China?" My brother prided himself on his historical knowledge of exotic cultures and vanished civilizations—a vestige of his Ivy League education. His film scripts were full of arcane allusions, most of which went over the audience's head. Here was an opportunity to show off, his moment to shine.

Pascal rewarded him with a smile. "The Vietnamese were tribal peoples. The Khmer in the south, the Cham here on the coast, the Montagnards in the highlands, the Hmong in the north. I am telling you only the largest ones. You can imagine that these peoples did not get along, and invaders took advantage of the divisions and disorder to dominate us. A thousand years of Chinese rule, a century as a colonial possession of the French."

"And now it's our turn," quipped my brother.

"Come now," our compatriot admonished, "you know there's no comparison between us and the French. We're not trying to build a colonial empire in Asia."

"Aren't we? Tell that to the Filipinos." Gray turned to Pascal. "I'll bet you're tired of Americans already, aren't you?"

Diplomatically, our guide sidestepped the question. "Vietnam has survived as long as it has by absorbing the ways of its conquerors. Buddhism, Confucianism, and the dynastic traditions, these were brought by the Chinese. Many Chinese words have entered Vietnamese, and the greatest works of our literature were composed in Chinese characters, the *chu nom.*

"Chinese characters?" Jakub was confused. "But I've seen Vietnamese written. You use a Latin script like ours."

"The French romanized Vietnamese writing, but *chu nom* came first. Before the thirteenth century, we had only an oral tradition. The *truyen*, our folk literature, was passed down verbally, like Homer."

Gray perked up at this mention of the Greek bard. "You know Homer, do you?"

"Bah!" Pascal made a noise of displeasure, a sound only a Frenchman could produce, exhaling his breath through pursed lips. "I taught the *Iliad* and the *Odyssey* at my lycée. In Greek."

"Did you really? Homeric Greek is so much harder than Attic Greek. I never mastered it," my brother admitted.

"But you must try harder!" Our guide launched into a lecture on the genius of Homer, one he must have delivered many times in front of his pupils, the sluggish ones who needed to apply themselves. "Do you think the treasures of civilization will be handed to you, like gifts? No, my friend, you must work to prove yourself worthy of them."

I caught Jakub's eye. He seemed to be having the same difficulty I was, maintaining a straight face through this dressing down. Gray genuinely loved the classics, but not enough, evidently, to satisfy a stern schoolmaster like Pascal.

"What about the treasures of your own literary tradition?" said my husband in a transparent attempt to change the subject.

Our guide took the bait. "Ah, have you heard of *The Tale of Kiêu*?" We shook our heads. "She is a poem composed here in Huế, by a scholar in the court of Gia Long."

"Here, did you say? How fascinating," my brother exclaimed. "Do you know it by heart?" He himself was fond of reciting poems from memory and was always looking to add to his repertoire.

"Alas, I do not. *The Tale of Kiêu* is an epic, like the *Odyssey*. She is very long and very sad. But I will tell you the story if you would like."

I knew that Gray would have liked nothing better than to hear the story in its entirety, but now it was our compatriot's turn to remind us that he'd paid for a tour of the Imperial City, not a lecture on Vietnamese literature. Ostentatiously, he glanced at his watch. "How much longer is this going to take, anyhow? I've got an appointment in town this afternoon."

"Monsieur!" The stern schoolmaster had returned. Reaching inside his jacket pocket, our guide extracted the

American's money and held it out as if it were contaminated. "Here are your dollars. I will thank you to leave the tour."

The man refused the refund. "Hey, I didn't mean to make you sore."

Pascal opened his hand and the bills fluttered to the ground. Abruptly, he turned his back on the four of us and started across the bridge. Watching his rigid figure depart, I worried he'd think that all Americans were as uncouth as this blond fellow. Without a moment's hesitation, I followed him and was gratified when Jakub and Gray did likewise. Looking back over my shoulder as we mounted the stone steps, I saw our compatriot stoop to collect his money off the paving stones before making his way out of the enclosure. Good riddance.

Our guide seemed embarrassed when we caught up with him outside the building. "I think maybe I am not so good with the tourists," he apologized. "I should not have lost my temper, but *The Tale of Kiêu* is very precious to Vietnamese people. Everyone knows it. Village farmers, shopkeepers, the beggars in the street. You ask them, and they will say it to you, and perhaps as well their favorite part."

"You don't want that kind of tourist," my brother reassured him. "Please, tell us the story."

Pascal beamed. "With pleasure. Kiêu is a beautiful girl from a good family, educated, an artist. Everyone admires her, but fate is not kind to Kiêu. Her father, he loses his money, and she is forced to give up her true love and marry a wicked man. Then she is sold into prostitution. Wherever she turns for help, she is betrayed. She finds a new husband, Từ Hải, a warrior king. He is very dear to her, *très cher*, but he is killed—"

"*New* husband! What about her first love?" It was one thing to be forced into marriage, but to give your heart away

26

to someone else? Perhaps I'd heard him incorrectly. Surely the Vietnamese didn't admire a heroine who was unfaithful.

"One must not judge Kiêu for seizing whatever small bit of happiness she can find," said our guide. "She is only human, *n'est-ce pas?*"

He was right. Which of us would not have done as she did? I reached for Jakub's hand and gave it a reassuring squeeze. Like Kiêu, he'd had no choice when misfortune struck except to carry on. I couldn't fill the empty place inside him, all I could do was love him. But what of poor Gray? I stole a glance at my brother. Thirty-nine and as far as I knew, he'd never been loved by anyone for more than a night or two. Back home it was too risky. McCarthy was going after homosexuals with only slightly less gusto than he pursued Communists; "buggery" was still a crime in England as well. Yet here with us on the production of *The Quiet American*, Michael Redgrave was living openly with his lover, Fred Sadoff. The two of them had adjoining rooms at the Majestic and were inseparable, both on the set and off, because Fred was playing the role of Dominguez, Fowler's assistant. Hiring him had been a condition of Michael's involvement.

Earlier that morning, we'd watched them board their flight to Cambodia while we waited to board ours to Huế. Tân Sơn Nhất airport was very small and there was only one lounge. I wondered if you had to be as famous as Michael Redgrave to be able to travel openly with your homosexual lover, or whether the greater license had to do with being in Vietnam. It wasn't the sort of question I could ask our guide outright, but I got my answer in a roundabout way.

After touring the Citadel and the Imperial City, we were supposed to take a dragon boat up the Perfume River to visit a Buddhist pagoda, but by the time we'd retraced our steps through the Purple Forbidden City, it was raining heavily. Pascal proposed taking a taxi instead, which would save us time.

"We might even visit Emperor Khải Định's tomb, if you are interested. He is very . . . unique."

"The emperor or the tomb?" said Gray.

Our guide laughed. "*Tous les deux.*" Both. The emperor's flamboyant style was reflected in the design of his tomb.

"Who was Khải Định?" Jakub wanted to know.

"He was probably Bảo Đại's father." *Probably?* Pascal seemed to be playing with us. "It is rumored that Bảo Đại was adopted. Emperor Khan Dinh liked boys."

A matter-of-fact statement. I couldn't imagine anyone in America speaking so frankly of a late leader's unconventional sexual habits.

Da Nang, a three-hour train ride from Huế, had everything you could ask for in a resort: wide, sandy beaches, elegant accommodations, fine restaurants, and far too few tourists, now that the French no longer controlled Vietnam. I was looking forward to doing absolutely nothing but swimming, sun bathing, and eating fresh seafood.

"You will enjoy Tourane," said our guide, using the French name for the port city. He'd insisted on accompanying us to the train station and supervising the purchase of three first-class tickets. While Gray and Jakub went to retrieve our bags from left luggage, where we'd deposited them on our way from the airport before setting off on our tour, Pascal showed me a stall right outside the entrance to the station where I could buy food for the journey. He recommended a sandwich called a *bánh mì*, seasoned meat mixed with Asian vegetables and herbs served in a French baguette. Assembling the *bánh mì* was a lengthy process, slicing the bread, layering the various elements inside, topping the filling with a spoonful of sauce, and then wrapping each sandwich carefully in brown paper. It was fortunate that the rain had tapered off, or Pascal and I would have gotten soaked through, waiting for the vendor to finish.

"There you are, *najdroższa*. It's time we—" My husband's attention was caught, momentarily, by the arrival of a pedicab. The canopy was up and from where I was standing, all I could see were a slender pair of trousered legs, the bottoms tucked into scuffed black army boots. The passenger emerged, a striking blonde carrying a military-style rucksack, a camera slung around her neck. She paid the driver, pulling the bills from a wallet she kept in her back pocket, just like a man, and checking the seat one last time to make sure she'd left nothing behind. Then she turned to face us, her blue eyes widening, surprise giving way to pure delight as she recognized Jakub.

"Cloud! *Je suis tellement content de te revoir.*"

"Mouche," he said. There were tears in his eyes as he moved to take her by the shoulders, kissing her, French-style, on either cheek, then standing back to get her measure. "*Chère* Mouche." He swiped at his eyes with the back of his hand.

I was too stunned to speak. *Mouche*? The French word for fly? And did I hear her address him in English, as cloud? Intimate nicknames: who was she, an old girlfriend? Why hadn't Jakub mentioned her? She was gorgeous, and chic, even wearing khaki pants and combat boots. How did French women manage it? All of these questions were whirling distressingly through my head. Meanwhile, Jakub and

"Mouche" were tossing sentences back and forth in rapid French. Pascal followed their conversation with interest, but they spoke too fast for me to pick up more than a word or two. *Gaulliste. France libre. Parti communiste. Fresnes.* It was Gray who had the presence of mind, finally, to ask if we might be introduced.

"Forgive me." Shyly, my husband presented his acquaintance to us with a bow. "I'm afraid Mouche will have to introduce herself. I never learned her real name."

# CHAPTER FOUR

## Tourane

"Laurence Bevillard." The woman held out her hand for each of us to shake in turn, Pascal, Gray, and me. "*Enchanté*," said our guide. "Tran Van Pascal." He inclined his head toward Jakub, including Mouche in the gesture. "*Vous etiez résistants, tous les deux?*" He was asking if they'd been in the Resistance.

"*Oui.*"

I realized my mistake. My husband had disguised himself as a seminary student during the war; Claude (pronounced like "cloud") Lassegue was the name on the false passport he'd used—he'd shown it to me—and "Mouche" must have been Laurence's *nom de guerre*. Could I assume they had not been romantically involved, since they hadn't divulged their true identities to one another in all the time they'd been working side by side? Surely it was a good sign that she hadn't flinched when, after revealing his real name, Jakub introduced me as his wife. He'd spoken in French, but Laurence responded in English, including me in the conversation by way of acknowledging my claim on her former comrade, which was kind of her.

"But she has not your name."

"Cara's an actress," he explained. "She goes by her maiden name."

Laurence nodded. "Yes, it is better, I think," she said amiably. "I too keep my name for my work."

"*Donc tu es aussi mariée?*"

"*Plus maintenant.*"

She was no longer married, she'd said in response to my husband's question. Switching once again to English, she explained that her work as a journalist came first. She'd been sent to cover the war in Indochina when it still looked as if the French could win and stayed on through the battle of Điện Biên Phủ, parachuting in with the First Airborne Group in a Flying Boxcar, "a gift from your government," she told Gray. She'd transferred all of her attention to my brother, whether out of consideration for me or because she found him handsome, as most women did, his devilish good looks enhanced by the goatee, it was impossible to tell. For her sake, I hoped it was the former. I couldn't help admiring Mouche. There seemed to be nothing she couldn't do, and yet she was entirely without conceit. Under different circumstances, we might have become friends.

"*Toujours intrépide,*" said Jakub. He'd called her fearless, and all she did was laugh. But why did he insist on speaking to her in French? Regardless of whether they'd been lovers, they shared a bond those two, and I felt left out.

"Laurence!" A trio of middle-aged Frenchman disembarked from a taxi and began making their way along the pavement toward us. They looked dapper in their light linen suits, each of them bearing a small leather portmanteau.

"How sweet," remarked Gray, "a matched set."

Everything went by quickly from that moment on— introductions all around, paying Pascal and thanking him for showing us the sights in Huế, boarding the train and finding our respective compartments—but in the flurry, I did manage to grab hold of a few details. Laurence's companions were bankers. They were all traveling to Da Nang for a trade show, the bankers to preside over the financial end of things, Laurence to write it up for *Le Journal d'Extrême Orient*. The event was being held in the center of town, whereas our resort was on the coast, making it unlikely that we'd see them again, which suited me just fine.

Surprisingly, and reassuringly, it suited Jakub just fine too. He'd become uncharacteristically formal, once the bankers arrived, his French suddenly encumbered with flowery turns of phrase, archaic expressions I'd learned in school but had never once heard uttered in casual conversation. He appeared intimidated in their presence, which I found baffling. They were more annoying than intimidating to me, French versions of the studio executives Father used to entertain at the lodge: magnanimous toward lesser mortals in a *noblesse obligé* kind of way, provided you acknowledged their superior status. Father'd had no choice but to play the game if he wanted to keep making pictures, but the French bankers had nothing Jakub wanted. Was he trying to impress Laurence? Why bother? It was obvious that she respected him already, and for reasons that had nothing to do with politeness.

I was still pondering the transformation in my husband as our train pulled out of the station. It was an old steam locomotive with a brass engine and a tall smokestack. The standard cars were made of wood and seemed pretty spartan, but first class was luxurious: plush upholstery, shutters on the windows to block the sun, and a ceiling fan to keep us cool. The three of us settled in for the journey with the newspapers and magazines we had purchased in the station's kiosk, but the view was so fascinating none of us did much reading.

Hué and its outskirts looked very much like the poorer

sections of London you saw from the train window coming into King's Cross, rows of houses built right up to the tracks, laundry hanging in the tiny yards. True, the houses were made of cement instead of brick, with corrugated tin roofs and canvas awnings for shade, and there were palm trees in some of the yards. Many homes had businesses on the ground floor, a bicycle repair shop or a little one-room grocery, with the family living on top. When the train slowed at a level crossing, I got a glimpse of a woman in one of the dwellings hunched over a portable stove stirring a pot, the room lit by a single lightbulb dangling from the ceiling.

Over the course of the journey, I compiled an entire album of picturesque scenes in my head: flooded rice paddies being worked by hand, farmers steering plows behind water buffalo, harbors filled with round fishing boats that looked like floating bowls, slender oars resting on the rim like chopsticks. I couldn't figure out how they steered in a straight line, with no prow to cut through the water. Best of all were the views of the craggy coast from high up in the mountains. Low clouds lent the scene a dreamy quality, like in a watercolor landscape, sea and sky blurring so you couldn't tell where one ended and the other began until, rounding a curve, you saw waves cresting along the shoreline, their edges limned by white foam. As the sun went down, the horizon turned the color of bruised plums.

Evening fell and the lights came on in our compartment. An attendant passed through the carriage with a cart, selling cigarettes and refreshments. We bought bottles of 33 Beer to go with our sandwiches, which turned out to be very tasty, but not easy to eat on a moving train. Our clothing was flecked with fragments of crust by the time we finished, our fingers sticky with errant sauce. We took turns visiting the toilet to wash up.

First class seemed to be reserved for Westerners, and I caught snatches of conversations being conducted in various European languages as I moved along the corridor. I'd brought my vanity bag and made an effort to repair my appearance. Our early start, combined with the hours spent touring the Imperial City in the rain, had left me looking disheveled, nothing a little makeup couldn't fix, but I was conscious of being at a disadvantage. Compared to the competition, I was pathetically unsophisticated, and no amount of eyeliner, powder, or lipstick, however skillfully applied, could change that.

The competition. Try as I might, I couldn't help regarding Laurence as my rival. The military garb, a variation on Marlene Dietrich's tuxedo, did not detract from the French journalist's allure. Quite the opposite. She was still feminine, deploying perfume, nail polish, and an upswept hairdo, artfully disarrayed, to attract her prey. Fly? She was the spider, entrapping men in her silky web. The bankers were completely smitten. Heading back to my seat, I heard a burst of laughter from their compartment, a woman's bell-like tones, clear notes sounding on a descending scale in counterpoint to an appreciative masculine chorus.

"*A Laurence!*" There was the sound of clinking glasses. They were toasting her. Of course they were.

Gray got to his feet as I slid open the door. "There you are! We were wondering if you'd been abducted and sold into white slavery."

"Not funny." I leaned down and gave Jakub a kiss. The next thing I knew, he'd pulled me into his lap and was returning the kiss with fervor, his tongue, his touch making me feel like the sexiest woman on earth. We were as eager as the first time we'd made love, although we'd learned a good deal about how to arouse one another in the months since. Just then, my beloved was stroking my hair, his fingertips sliding to the nape of my neck, pressing gently as I arched my body against his.

My brother coughed discreetly. "After I clean up, I think I'll head to the café car for a drink and a smoke." His voice seemed to come from far away. One last, lingering kiss before Jakub and I disentangled ourselves to sit primly across from one another, only our knees touching. I felt a bit guilty for driving Gray away, but I'd needed my husband's caresses. Parts of his life remained closed to me, grief-encrusted memories too tender to probe. As much as I wanted to know what Laurence had meant to him, I took comfort from his ardor. I would wait until Jakub was ready to open that door, and hopefully I wouldn't have to wait very long.

"So, we meet again!"

I looked up from my *Marie Claire* magazine, my view of the ocean blocked by a pair of plaid swimming trunks. It wasn't that they were large, but their wearer was standing close. Too close. Without waiting to be invited, our compatriot plopped himself down on a bamboo chaise lounge next to Gray.

"I don't think we introduced ourselves yesterday," he said, extending a hand. "Buckingham Polk."

"Buckingham, eh?" My brother struggled to keep a straight face. "I'll bet they called you 'Buck' in the fraternity."

"Why, yes. How did you—?"

36

"I knew a Buck at Yale. Not strictly speaking a fraternity boy. He was a Bonesman."

"Boola boola!"

Jakub and I exchanged glances. Did Yalies give off some kind of aura that enabled them to recognize one another? Wearing only a bathing suit and sunglasses, a hotel towel draped around his neck, our new acquaintance did not look especially patrician, yet Gray had pegged him instantly. Not only that, but the loutishness of the previous day had been forgotten. He and his fellow Ivy-Leaguer now seemed to be hitting it off.

"You're obviously referring to William Buckingham Staunton III." Our Buck seemed to take pleasure in sounding out every last syllable. "He was before my time, but some of the old boys got us confused because we had the same nickname. Senator's son from Connecticut, wasn't he?"

"Massachusetts."

"Imagine, meeting another Bonesman out here," mused our compatriot. "They do say we get around."

"Oh, I didn't mean to give you the impression that I belonged to Skull and Bones," my brother demurred. "Staunton and I were in the same college. We nearly got ourselves rusticated one year for a prank we pulled." Remembering, his eyes crinkled in amusement. "Lucky thing his father was a Fellow."

"Which college were you in?"

"Branford."

Buck hauled off and punched Gray on the shoulder. "Jonathan Edwards. Class of '47."

"Class of '40." My brother rubbed his shoulder. "I think we can put the traditional rivalry to rest, don't you?"

"Class of '40, you say?"

"That's right."

Buck did the calculation on his fingers. "Just missed you. I entered that fall, should have graduated in '44, but the Japs went and attacked Pearl Harbor my sophomore year. Went home at Christmastime and enlisted."

"Did you? Which branch?"

"Air Force."

"Same here," said Gray. "FMPU."

"FMPU? Now there's an acronym I've never heard, and I thought I knew them all."

"First Motion Picture Unit. We made propaganda films and training videos." He sighed. "I wanted to be a pilot, or a navigator at the very least. Guess I didn't have the right stuff."

"Neither did I, my friend. Neither did I," our compatriot consoled him. "They sent me to flight school in Louisiana and gave me a barrel of tests. I was on track to become a pilot until a stupid training accident ruined my chances of getting back in the air. Next thing I knew, they'd promoted me to captain and made me an instructor. Said they needed men like me to keep the pilots flying."

"Keep 'em flying. We made that film, you know." Gray's voice was flat, without a trace of pride.

Hijinks at Yale and the disappointments of his military career. I was learning things about my brother's younger days I'd never thought to question. What mischief had he gotten up to with the Massachusetts senator's son? I'd never known him to consort with anyone whose name came with a Roman numeral attached to it, but he seemed fond of his classmate, old William Buckingham Staunton III. How did this friendship square with the Gray I knew, the guy who'd contemplated fighting the fascists in Spain during this very same period? He'd been committed enough to the cause to get branded as pink, a premature anti-fascist if not a card-

38

carrying Communist. That's what led to the subpoena from HUAC, prompting our flight to England some five years earlier. He'd recently succeeded in clearing his name, but his sympathies remained with the poor and oppressed. I never heard him speak of the Brahmin set, to which the senator's son clearly belonged, with anything but disdain. And yet there was another, unexpected side to him as well. Not only had he signed up to fight for his country (for some reason, I'd always assumed he was drafted), but he'd had visions of himself as a hero, a fighter pilot as opposed to a mere enlisted man.

Gray didn't talk much about his wartime service and since I was only nine when he left for basic training, memories of that era were scant, but one scene stuck in my mind. Father kept a framed picture of my brother in uniform on his desk. Once, when he was home on leave, I'd observed him turn the photo face down—funny, how seemingly minor details turn out to have significance. I must have registered the gesture, stored it away someplace for later, when it would make sense. Had he been ashamed to wear the uniform, ashamed to be safe in California making films while other men his age were out there, doing brave deeds and dying? Here was something important I'd never suspected. Deep down, my brother was staunchly patriotic.

"Don't belittle your contribution to the war effort," said Buck. "There were plenty of unsung heroes working behind the scenes, as in any enterprise. I'd bet you were one of them. What's your name, anyhow?"

"Oh, sorry. Gray Walden. And this is my sister Cara and her new husband, Jakub."

"Newlyweds! Are you kids here on your honeymoon?"

He'd taken a liking to us "kids," never mind that he and

Jakub were virtually the same age. Before we could explain what had brought us to Vietnam, he'd summoned a strolling waiter and ordered a bottle of champagne. A vestige of the colonial era, the Da Nang beach was civilized, like the ones on the French Riviera. You could get anything you wanted with a snap of your fingers, and unlike the Riviera, it didn't cost an arm and a leg.

"You see? That's the beauty of this country," said Buck as we waited for the champagne to arrive. "It's got tremendous potential. With a little technical and economic assistance, the Vietnamese people will finally enter the modern age."

My husband raised himself on an elbow and turned toward him. "You are here to provide that assistance?"

"I am. And, let me tell you, the first step is to get rid of the French."

"You're not referring to the military, I take it."

Our compatriot gave a huff of exasperation. "They pulled out the last of their troops in June of last year. You'd have thought French businessmen would have gone with them. Some of the enterprises they're managing are in remote provinces. Mines and rubber plantations and the like. Grueling labor and they expect the coolies to keep working for peanuts—their word, not mine—all to enrich the owners. I don't see how they can expect to keep it up without armed protection."

"That's capitalism for you," said Gray. "Audacious to the last, so long as there's a profit to be made."

I glimpsed the waiter, returning. "Look, here's the bubbly!" It didn't seem fair to subject our new acquaintance to one of my brother's political diatribes when he'd been kind enough to splurge on champagne, particularly when Gray had been the one to draw him out. I'd have been content to bury myself back in my magazine. After the American's performance in Huế, I wanted nothing more to do with him, and it was apparent that Jakub felt the same way, but it was too fine a day to bear ill will toward anyone. The sun was strong, but a soft breeze blowing off the sea kept us from getting overheated as we lay on our chairs, listening to the music of the surf. I'd have been happy to remain in Da Nang for the remainder of our time in Vietnam.

Buck did the honors. "To York and Cara," he proclaimed, raising his glass in a toast.

"Ya-cob," my husband corrected.

"Ya-cob. What kind of name is that?"

"It's the Polish version of Jacob," I said. "Jakub Abramowicz."

"Polish, eh?" He turned to Gray and me. "But you must be Americans, with a good New England name like Walden."

My brother had no tolerance for nationalist stupidity, whether it emanated from the McCarthyite president of the Screen Actors Guild or a fellow Ivy League graduate. "Actually," he said, "our father's Hungarian. He changed his name to Walden for Hollywood. It used to be more like Jakub's, back in the old country."

I was watching Buck's face as he absorbed this information. To his credit, he was deeply ashamed. Mortified might not be too strong a word. He removed his sunglasses in order to blot his face with his towel. He had the pale complexion to match his blond hair and blue eyes and it was hard to tell whether he was sunburned or blushing, but his face was definitely red.

"Ah. Put my foot in it, didn't I?"

An awkward silence followed, during which time our compatriot downed his glass of champagne and insisted on topping up ours before refilling his own.

41

Jakub was the one to smooth things over. "My fondest wish is to become an American citizen."

"You already drive like a native," I laughed. "We were married in California in September, and you should have seen him on the L.A. freeway."

Buck grasped this opening like a drowning man. "So you're not on your honeymoon. It did surprise me, having your brother tagging along like a third wheel. What brings you to Vietnam?"

We explained about the production of *The Quiet American* and our various roles (or non-roles, in my case) on the set. It had been worrying me, how I would occupy myself for the remaining time in Saigon. But our new acquaintance came up with the perfect solution.

"Can you type?" he asked. "I could use a secretary."

# CHAPTER FIVE

## Grands Magasins Charner
## February 18, 1957

Not only did I type, I took dictation. The Wentworth Academy for Young Ladies equipped their graduates with a backup plan. Those who failed to find a wealthy husband, first time out, might prove themselves indispensable in the business world and end up marrying their boss. I hadn't fully bought into this scenario and my secretarial skills were not first rate, but they would do for Buck's purposes.

"*Najdroższa*, are you sure?" The sun had barely risen and we were both getting ready for work.

I turned so Jakub could help fasten the zipper on the back of my skirt. "Positive."

What else was I supposed to do for the next three weeks? Audie Murphy was back from Hong Kong, but he was still on bed rest and everyone was in a bad mood because they were losing precious days, scrambling to shoot around him. My husband would be putting in long hours with the crew, once Murphy was well, to make up for the weeks they'd lost; for now they had him doing odd jobs, such as hunting around various machine shops with one of Bill Hornbeck's technical assistants, attempting to replace the gear in a piece of equipment that had arrived damaged in shipment. He was learning his way around Saigon's back alleys and working-class districts where few tourists ventured.

I wasn't the sort to idle around the Majestic's pool, gossiping and playing mah-jongg with the other stray women attached to the production. I was looking forward to starting my new job. *Yes, Mr. Polk. I'll have it ready for your signature in no time at all. No, Mr. Polk. There are no messages.* I'd practiced sounding secretarial and just hoped that I remembered enough shorthand to carry it off.

Of course, in order to get in character, you need to look the part. Having met my employer on the beach, it was important, I felt, to establish myself as a professional. No more mistakes like on the set in Tây Ninh. I'd assembled a demure outfit from the wardrobe I'd brought with me to Vietnam, preparing for my new job the way I'd prepare for any role: a navy blue skirt topped with a conservative blouse and over it a little bolero jacket like Maggie McNamara's in *Three Coins in the Fountain*. She married the prince at the end of that picture, and I figured it couldn't hurt to model myself on the secretary she played, especially since I resembled her. Not that I had any designs on Buck, or anything to fear from that quarter. "Your bride will be well taken care of," he'd assured Jakub when we parted.

My husband looked at his watch. "It's half past seven. We've got time for Givral if you hurry."

One last glance in the mirror and we were off. I wasn't due at the office until ten that day, but a car would be coming for Jakub in an hour: ample time for a cup of coffee and a freshly baked croissant at the patisserie across the street. We both loved the place, which Graham Greene had immortalized in *The Quiet American*. He referred to it as the milk bar and it was where Fowler's Vietnamese mistress, Phuong, went for her daily milkshake. The tables were close together, just like in a French café, and the place was always crowded, even early in the morning. We were still scanning the room for a spot when I noticed Gray at a window table, lost in thought, a cup of coffee at his elbow. He sometimes went there to write, but he didn't seem to be in any condition to work. He looked unkempt, hair uncombed, his eyes bloodshot, wearing the same tan trousers and blue button-down shirt he'd been wearing the night before.

Jakub and I looked at one another, the same thought running through our heads. He must have gone out carousing after bidding us goodnight. Saigon offered an inconceivable range of sexual temptations; every taste was catered to, according to some of my husband's fellow crew members. While we'd used the time off to visit other parts of Vietnam, they'd explored the seedier parts of the city in search of illicit pleasures.

"Hey," I said, giving my brother a peck on the cheek as I took a seat beside him. "Don't you believe in sleep anymore?"

"Oh, yes. I believe fervently in sleep." He yawned and rubbed his eyes. "I worship sleep. Problem is, my downstairs neighbor's been having nightmares."

Jakub made a face. "I guess the Majestic isn't soundproofed very well, eh?"

"It's soundproofed perfectly well, for ordinary disruptions. The screaming didn't wake me, it was only afterwards I heard it."

"Afterwards? After what?" I said.

"After the shooting stopped."

"Shooting!" my husband and I exclaimed in unison.

Gray's downstairs neighbor turned out to be Audie

45

Murphy, who slept with a loaded revolver under his pillow, a practice he'd adopted in wartime when it was necessary, for self-preservation. He didn't feel safe in Vietnam, and one of the things he'd done in Hong Kong apparently was to stock up on ammunition.

"He fired eleven rounds into the ceiling. His bed must be directly beneath mine. I swear, I felt the reports through the mattress." He was wide awake after that, and unwilling to stay in his hotel room another night. Forlornly, he asked if we thought the Continental had any vacancies.

"I expect they do," said Jakub. "But you look like you need to get to bed right now."

While I ordered coffee and croissants for the two of us, he took Gray back across the street to get the key to our room from the desk clerk and to make sure my brother wouldn't be disturbed by the housekeeping staff. I watched him returning from this errand, his smile radiant. I could live on that smile and nothing else.

"We're in luck," he said, sliding into his seat. "Room 214's opening up."

"Room 214? Is that a deluxe room or something?" Our own room on the top floor was fairly small, but it had a balcony that looked onto rue Catinat where it was pleasant to sit in the evening.

"Room 214 is where Graham Greene stayed. It overlooks the square." He pointed out the window. "See it there, on the corner? Your brother will love it."

He was happy because he'd made Gray happy: my husband was uncommonly attuned to the feelings of others, a trait I associated with his sensitivity as a musician. Naturally it worked both ways. Often I could gauge his mood, when listening to him practice, small things like the way his bow lingered on the penultimate notes of a bar, his unwillingness to resolve a melancholy phrase suggesting that he was caught up in his memories from before the war. At such times, I'd learned that there was little I could say to bring him out of his blue funk, but I could go and sit quietly nearby, my presence a reminder that he was no longer alone. Keeping company at the end of the world, I called it.

"I wish we knew more about this Buck fellow," said Jakub. "What exactly is he doing in Vietnam?"

"The American?" My brother had christened him with the title—playing off Fowler's name for Pyle in *The Quiet American*—and we'd all taken to using it. "He's a businessman." I buttered a piece of croissant, smeared it with apricot jam, and popped the flaky pastry into my mouth.

"Yes, *najdroższa*." My husband paused in the middle of buttering his own croissant, knife poised. "But what sort of businessman?" He made a dismissive motion with the knife. "He's hired you to work in a makeshift office in an empty building without a clue as to what you'll be doing. Do you think that's normal?"

I didn't want to admit it, but I shared his misgivings. Immediately upon our return from Da Nang on Friday, we'd gone, the two of us, to locate the address the American had provided. A narrow three-story structure, the building was a short walk from our hotel and just a few steps from Ben Thanh Market, its entrance wedged between a bar and a dry cleaner's. We'd climbed the stairs to the second floor, coming out on an L-shaped corridor with doors on either side, all closed, save for one at the far end, at the hinge where the corridor turned.

"Do you think that's his office?" I whispered, spooked by the empty silence. Saigon was a noisy, crowded city. The hush inside Buck's building was unearthly. No sounds of typing emanated from behind those closed doors, no conversations or signs of industry, let alone habitation. Making our way to the open office, our footsteps echoed down the hallway. Whoever was in there could have heard us coming a mile off and, sure enough, before we reached the turn in the corridor, my new employer poked his head out the door.

"Oh, hello." He was wearing business attire: dark trousers, a white shirt with the sleeves rolled up, polished shoes. Peeking in, I saw a suit jacket draped over the back of a metal office chair, a neatly rolled tie on the desk next to a telephone and a typewriter. There were crates and cartons on the floor, crumpled newspaper littering every surface. We'd interrupted him in the middle of setting up.

Jakub cleared his throat. "Sorry for intruding. I just wanted to make sure we had the correct address—"

"Ha!" Buck gave a bark of laughter. "You wanted to check me out. Well, come in and have a look around. It's a mess at the moment, but I'll have the place in shape by Monday morning."

Stepping aside, he ushered us into "the suite," as he called it, a rather grand designation for the three shabby rooms he was renting. The central room, the one we'd entered, was his office and it was pretty spacious. To its left was a windowless storeroom cluttered with random pieces of furniture—bookcases, a coat rack, a standing lamp, filing cabinets, and metal wastebaskets—clunky, nondescript items, the sort of decor you'd see in a downbeat 1940s detective movie. Apparently they'd come with the place, as did the rickety Venetian blinds that covered the windows of Buck's office. A connecting door led from his domain to mine, a tiny room off to the right. It had its own entrance off the corridor and a window but was barely large enough for the three of us to occupy at the same time. Buck had moved in an aluminum typing table and a straight-backed chair. That was it.

"Oh," I said, unable to hide my dismay. Although he kept his mouth shut, Jakub's face wore an I-told-you-so expression.

"It needs a woman's touch," the American apologized. "I'm afraid I'm no good at decorating."

True to his word, when I showed up that Monday morning for my first day of work, Buck was waiting to escort me to the Grands Magasins Charner, a big French department store in the center of Saigon where I was to have *carte blanche* to purchase anything we needed to make the place more inviting.

"Anything, Mr. Polk?" I thought it best to start out on the right foot, addressing him formally, as the respectful employee I intended to be.

"Just so long as I can justify it on my expense account, Miss Walden," he replied with a wink. The pale lashes came down, one eyelid closed, but the other eye remained fixed in place. It was glass, I realized, trying not to stare.

Thankfully, Buck seemed not to notice my impoliteness, his mind being elsewhere. My mind was elsewhere too. An expense account meant that he worked for somebody else. I was thinking that Jakub would be reassured to know that this was not a one-man operation, although I was still in the dark as to precisely what kind of operation it was. Hopefully I'd know more by the end of the day. Sooner or later, I'd be given something to do. He couldn't be paying me fifty dollars a week to sit at my desk and file my nails, could he?

"Be careful!" The American grabbed my arm and yanked me away from the curb. A scooter taking the corner too fast plowed straight across the section of pavement where I'd been standing. But for Buck's quick reflexes, I'd have been run over.

"They drive like maniacs in this country," he said, shaking his head. "I promised your husband I'd look after you."

Not every man would take his pledge so seriously. "Thank you."

We'd come to the Bùng Binh traffic circle, a busy intersection with a fountain in the middle. The Grands Magasins Charner occupied the better part of a block at its western end. You got a good view of the fountain from the sidewalk in front of the department store, and an important scene in the movie would be shot there. I knew this from Gray. He'd shown us all the key locations on our first day in Saigon, and I'd been meaning to get back and have a look inside the building—he said it was absolutely stunning, rivaling Harrods in London or the Galeries Lafayette in Paris.

Gray was wrong. Harrods and the Galeries Lafayette had nothing on the Grands Magasins Charner. Those stores might be larger, but neither of them had a mosaic staircase curling through the main room. Blue tiles swirled upwards to a landing designed in intricate patterns, stars and crescents picked out in ochre, beige, and maroon. Grasping the railing as we climbed to the furniture department on the second floor, I had the impression of being on a Mediterranean cruise, looking out over some sun-drenched North African port. Like the Tourane resort, the elegance of the French colonial era was on full display. No detail was neglected. The banisters were brass, a rooster topped the bottommost one, his beak open as if he were crowing, and there were other whimsical touches throughout the emporium. Unlike

Harrods or the Galeries Lafayette, whoever designed the store had a sense of humor.

This was a place to linger, if you had money to spend. The merchandise all seemed to have been imported and was fairly pricey, but Buck didn't seem to mind. We selected rugs and wall hangings for both rooms, a small desk with matching chair for my office, a mahogany conference table with six chairs to supplement the furniture in his, these new items suggesting that Buck intended to have people in. I imagined meetings where I might be asked to take notes—at last, an indication of my duties! We had yet to discuss specifics. I knew only my salary, and that I'd be working from eight to four, with half an hour for lunch, but now I seized the opening he'd given me.

"If you don't mind, Mr. Polk, I'd like to know what you've hired me to do." There, I'd said it. Would he give me a straightforward answer? For a long moment he was silent and I feared I'd be playing mah-jongg by the pool after all. At least it would only be for a few weeks, I consoled myself. I could catch up on my reading, swim laps, work on my tan. By the time we returned to touring with the trio, I'd be fit, mentally and physically.

"Miss Walden," he said finally, "I apologize for not being more forthcoming about the job. I've only recently arrived in Vietnam myself and I'm still getting the lay of the land. There's a lot to learn. As for your responsibilities, I've never had to hire my own secretary. I inherited my last one from a predecessor and, to be frank, I depended on her to teach me the ropes. The office furniture won't be delivered until the end of the afternoon. If you'd like to join me for lunch, I'll do my best to explain our operation here."

I laughed, disarmed by his honesty, and relieved that I would not be consigned to the mah-jongg tiles after all.

"I've never been anyone's secretary. I guess we'll both be learning as we go along."

We descended the mosaic staircase to the restaurant, another vestige of imperial France. Beneath glittering chandeliers, well-coiffed European ladies nibbled sandwiches and sipped tea from delicate porcelain cups, attended by waiters in uniform, middle-aged Vietnamese men whose outward reserve could not mask their pride at having attained a position here, in the great emporium's inner sanctum.

Buck was the only man in the room under the age of sixty and, as such, attracted inordinate interest from the other patrons. I noticed a nervous tic in his right eye (the good eye) as he studied the menu. He seemed ill at ease in the surroundings, his athletic body more accustomed to the masculine, leather armchairs of a gentleman's club than to a frou frou tearoom.

"The people are very rude here," I said. "Would you like to go somewhere else?"

"Oh, we don't need to do that."

I realized that I needed to be more assertive, more like the take-charge secretary he was used to. Picking up my handbag, I rose to leave, motioning that he should follow. A waiter appeared, flustered.

"*Vous avez besoin de quelque chose, M'sieur, M'dame?*"

"*Nous sommes désolés,*" I apologized without halting in my progress toward the exit. There was nothing we needed except privacy, and I knew where we could find it: a noodle shop on a side street half a block from the Continental. The place was clean enough, the food was good, and few Westerners frequented it. Jakub had discovered it on one of his expeditions and we'd already been there twice.

Buck approved of my choice. "You certainly know your

way around this city, Miss Walden." He ate most of his meals at the American Club, but he was game to try the local fare. While he chose a table, I went up to the counter to order. A bowl of pho, steaming hot noodle soup with beef or chicken, was surprisingly refreshing in the middle of the day, although I couldn't bring myself to eat it for breakfast, as the Vietnamese did. Cold spring rolls filled with shrimp, basil, mint, cilantro and lettuce and topped with a spicy peanut sauce were a house specialty, and we could round out our lunch with Vietnamese iced coffee.

While we waited for the food to arrive, the American gave me an overview of his business. He called himself an economic planner, applying Western know-how to Vietnamese industries, from agriculture to manufacturing and commerce. As the French departed (although they weren't divesting themselves of their enterprises as rapidly as he would have liked), it was natural for our country to step in. We had the expertise to reorganize the burgeoning enterprises, to bring them in line with the most up-to-date, efficient practices. America also had the capital to invest in improvements. Buck's firm connected local entrepreneurs with eager investors back home.

"In other words, you're here to make money?" I tried to maintain a neutral tone, but couldn't help imagining my brother's reaction when he learned that my new job entailed bolstering the fortunes of American financiers.

"There's nothing wrong with making money," he said, "but we're talking about freedom, Miss Walden. Little Vietnam needs our help to become a democracy. Hồ Chí Minh is in league with the Soviets and the Red Chinese. He's turning North Vietnam into a Communist dictatorship. It's up to America to make sure Free Vietnam doesn't go that route."

I knew what Gray would say to that. I'd heard him say it in this very restaurant at dinner the night before: America should have been on the side of the Vietnamese people all along, not propping up a decaying colonial regime. If Hồ Chí Minh turned to our enemies for help in the struggle for liberation, this was because we'd left him no other choice. And now we were backing a leader in the South who seemed every bit as dictatorial as his Communist counterpart in the North, a man who commanded even less loyalty from his countrymen.

"You disagree, Miss Walden?"

I must have been frowning. When would I learn to keep a poker face in these situations?

"Shouldn't we be helping the Vietnamese conduct free elections?" I said, parroting my brother. "It's their country, after all, and that's what the parties agreed to in Geneva, isn't it?" The division of the country into North and South was supposed to be temporary. The Geneva Accords had called for elections to be held in 1956. Voters from both regions were supposed to choose a single government to unite the entire country. But President Diem had cancelled the elections and the United States hadn't objected.

Buck's response came out so smoothly, it was evident he'd anticipated my questions. "The United States never signed that agreement, and do you know why? We didn't want to hold the Vietnamese to an artificial timetable. These poor people have been oppressed so long, they aren't ready to govern themselves. They'll vote for the Communists because they're starving and they don't know any better. Communism thrives on misery. If you've got nothing to lose, why not bring the whole system crashing down? The best way to promote democracy is to make this country prosperous. In a strong economy, unemployment is low, wages are high, and nobody starves. Economic development is what Vietnam needs. Planning, education, technical training, combined with aid, of course, but only enough to get the country on its feet. We don't want the Vietnamese to become dependent on us for handouts. We do want them to have something worth defending, something of their own to be proud of, enterprises they built with their own hands. I'm here to make that possible, with your help."

Was it really so simple? Years of listening to Gray rail against capitalist greed made me skeptical, but the American struck me as sincere. Working for him would be interesting, if nothing else, and I was flattered that he took my opinions seriously, as my husband and brother did not. Always, I was the one struggling to catch up when the conversation turned to politics. Lacking Gray's education, or Jakub's hard-won experience, I couldn't pretend to know the world as well as they did, but that didn't mean I had nothing to offer. Here was an opportunity to learn about conditions in this part of the world while doing my bit to improve them.

Our pho arrived and I showed Buck how to eat it. First I tried a spoonful of broth, to check the seasonings. I liked things tangy, and added a squeeze of lime, along with bean sprouts and a few basil leaves. These ingredients were served on a separate plate, allowing you to suit your own taste. There were also raw slices of chili peppers and a bowl of pungent fish sauce, neither of which I was daring enough to try.

"What's in those two bottles?"

"Those are dipping sauces. The dark one's sweet and the red one's spicy. You can mix them in that little dish in front of you and add them to the soup." I demonstrated, using mostly the dark sauce, with just a tiny speck of the red one. "Vietnamese people do it fifty-fifty, but I tried it that way and it made my eyes water."

Buck proved to be far more adventuresome than I was, adding peppers, fish sauce, and a healthy dash of the spicy condiment to the broth in his bowl.

"Whew," he said, after his first mouthful, "you weren't kidding!" He downed a glass of water in one long swallow. I expected him to push the pho aside and concentrate on the spring rolls, but he dutifully finished the soup before moving on to the next course. He waited until the coffee arrived before resuming the conversation.

"We're starting from scratch, Miss Walden, and I must say, it's proving more difficult to break into this market than I'd expected." The trade show that brought Laurence and the bankers to Da Nang had brought him to the coastal city as well, but he'd found himself sidelined early on, unable to get a single one of the budding Vietnamese entrepreneurs in the hall to hear him out in the presence of the French. Hence his retreat to the beach.

"There I was, prepared to invest American dollars in their businesses." He shook his head in disbelief. "American dollars."

I made a sympathetic noise. American currency was accepted everywhere in Saigon, and you got the black market rate of 105 piastres to the dollar, as opposed to the official exchange rate, which was less than a third of that. It was hard to imagine anyone turning Buck down if he was waving dollars in their face, but he'd since learned that French banks maintained tight control over business transactions in Vietnam.

"We're going to try a different strategy, bypass the French and go straight to the source."

"The source?" I stirred up the thick layer of condensed milk in the bottom of my glass, to blend it with the rich, dark coffee. You didn't need sugar, the milk was so sweet. Vietnamese iced coffee was one thing I was going to miss, once we were back in Europe.

My employer rested his elbows on the table and leaned closer, as if to impart a secret, although he didn't lower his voice. "Miss Walden, do you have any idea how many Catholics from Red Vietnam are living in the South right now?"

"Close to a million, isn't it?" I'd picked up this statistic from Pascal in Huế.

"What an asset you're going to be!" he said, beaming. "Close to a million, yes, and anti-Communist, every last one of them. The government is working overtime, trying to get them resettled. Believe you me, it isn't easy. They fled for their lives, as you know, brought nothing with them except the clothes on their backs. First thing is to get them housed and fed, but then what?"

I took a swallow of coffee. "I'm afraid I don't know, Mr. Polk."

"Work, Miss Walden. The refugees need work, and we're in the position to provide it." Buck proceeded to outline his plan. His outfit would go to the villages where they were living, connect with local leaders to set up enterprises: road-building, bridge-building, railroads, canals. Better transportation networks meant that food grown in the countryside could be sold in the cities. Under the French, Vietnam imported too much and exported too little. Rice and salt, for example: the country possessed the capacity to produce far more of these essentials than it currently did, but there had to be a more efficient way to get them to market. The French hadn't been interested in developing the export trade, however, seeing the colony as nothing more than a milk cow—I noted the word—for their own profit.

My eyes began to glaze over. "Maybe we should continue the conversation at the office," I suggested. We needed to move the old furniture back into the storeroom to free up space before our new purchases were delivered. Also, I needed to use the lavatory and didn't trust the restaurant's. While Buck summoned the waiter, I excused myself to go back to the Continental. I'd intended to use the ladies' room off the lobby, but when I passed by the reception desk, I noticed that our key was back in its alcove, so I went to the room to freshen up. Gray must have been able to move into his own room.

Buck was waiting downstairs. "What should we call ourselves, Miss Walden?" he asked as we walked to the office. "Our company needs a name."

"Surely you have something in mind, Mr. Polk." Here I was, a temporary employee still foggy about the details of her job, being asked to come up with a name for the entire business. Try as I might, I couldn't convince myself that the American's enterprise was aboveboard.

"Well, I've got an idea," he admitted, "but it's no good."

"Let's hear it."

He mumbled something I couldn't make out. As in the Mediterranean countries I knew, where life came to a standstill in the heat of the day, Saigon slowed down from noon until about three. The streets were empty of traffic, the sidewalks free of pedestrians. I should have been able to hear him.

"What did you say?"

"The Flora Trade Alliance."

"Flora, as in flora and fauna? I'm not sure I understand the significance."

"It's my mother's name." He was blushing. Either that, or the heat was getting to him; it was hard to tell which, it was so hot and he was so fair-skinned.

"Your mother's name," I repeated. A part of me wanted to laugh, another part was touched, but mostly I was baffled that "our company" could be so ad hoc. The American was prepared to travel throughout South Vietnam, passing out dollars to entrepreneurial refugees. He had an unlimited budget, and no administrative oversight from what I could tell. Who was funding him and why didn't they want their name going on the letterhead? I could no longer push aside my apprehension. Something was off, and I had a pretty good idea what it was. Graham Greene's quiet American worked for the CIA. Did Buck?

I wished Jakub were with me. Jakub, with his wartime aptitude for subterfuge, had instantly seen through the surface charm of a Soviet spy we'd encountered in Budapest during the failed Hungarian revolution. We'd taken advantage of a lull in the fighting to track down a missing relative and bring him out. The spy was on our tail and monitoring our every move. Had it not been for Jakub's well-honed instincts, we wouldn't have made it out ourselves before the Soviets came back and crushed the uprising.

But this was different. If Buck was a spy, at least he was one of ours. That thought should have been reassuring, but somehow it wasn't. I might be in no immediate danger, working for him, and yet the prospect of being employed, even indirectly, by the United States government—the same government that had hounded my brother out of the country—made me uneasy. And having me as his secretary might pose problems for Buck, down the road. What would Uncle Sam say, I wondered, if it came out that he'd hired the sister of a "Red," a man who'd chosen exile in

England to avoid naming names? For all the government knew, both of us could be in league with the Soviet Union.

"I told you it wasn't any good," said Buck.

The poor man. All this time I'd been worrying about his clandestine affiliations, he was looking for my approval. Such vulnerability in a man his age made him an unlikely spy. Either that, or he wasn't a very good one.

"Sorry, I was thinking about something else. Flora's a fine name for the company."

Buck blushed with pleasure. "Do you really think so?" He held the door, allowing me to enter the building first. One thing for certain, Flora Polk had instilled good manners in her son.

"I do. It's sweet, naming your business after your mother." I paused at the entrance to the stairwell and confronted him. "But what will your investors think of it?"

"My investors?"

"The people back home who are putting up the money for this enterprise you're starting," I called over my shoulder, mounting the stairs. "Shouldn't they get a say in what the company's called?"

"Oh, yes. The investors. They don't bother with minor details. They're busy people."

He couldn't lie to save his life. The second floor was as deserted as the day before, but I waited until we were in the office before pressing him further.

"Who are you working for, Mr. Polk?"

I'd expected Buck to play dumb, but he surprised me. "You're nobody's fool, are you?" He chuckled, pleased as punch. "Of course, I'd expect nothing less from a young lady who not only exposed a Communist spy operating out of the American embassy in Budapest, but had a hand in his capture."

Taken aback, at first all I could do was stare (but I avoided looking at the glass eye). "Well," I said, finding my voice. "I guess that answers my question."

# CHAPTER SIX

## The Cimarron Kid

Why didn't I quit? I couldn't come up with a single reason, not one that would satisfy Gray and Jakub. Walking back to the Continental, I dreaded telling them that I was actually employed by some arm of the US government and that, knowing this, I'd agreed to stay on. My brother would say I was compromising myself, putting capitalist interests above the needs of the Vietnamese people. He'd said as much even before he knew for sure what Buck was up to, and the American hadn't denied that he was here to make money. The Vietnamese might see some of the profits, but the lion's share would go to Buck's investors back in the United States.

"Can someone do the right thing for the wrong reason?" I asked my husband over gin slings on the terrace.

"Is that a rhetorical question?"

I poked at the ice in my glass with a swizzle stick. "Buck told me why he's here. There's a group that calls themselves the American Friends of Vietnam. They sponsored a conference in Washington last summer and some young senator gave a speech that really inspired him."

"The American Friends of Vietnam? I've never heard of them. Who are they?"

I tried to recollect what the American had told me.

"They're part of the ICA, I think."

"The ICA? I've never heard of them either. Do you mean the IRC?"

"I'm not sure. What do they do?"

"The IRC is a humanitarian relief organization," said Jakub. "They helped get Jewish refugees out of France after Germany occupied the country. They also sent aid to West Berlin during the blockade and they're doing a good deal these days to get Hungarian refugees resettled."

I seized my opening. "That's what Buck's doing! His agency is working to resettle the North Vietnamese refugees in villages throughout Free Vietnam. They're sending volunteers to build houses and schools and hospitals. Then they'll train the people in the most up-to-date practices, to help them become self-sufficient."

"I see." He sounded skeptical.

We'd be traveling together to some of the villages, to oversee their progress and lend a hand when required. One of the things the American had shown me, while we waited for the furniture to arrive, was an inventory drawn up by a missionary couple in Biên Hòa listing the needs of the communities they served, everything from clothing, food, bedding, and cooking utensils to water buffalo, agricultural machinery, and seeds. The Catholic Relief Office in Saigon was able to provide the majority of these items—including the water buffalo. His job was to procure the rest and transport them to the villages in trucks supplied by the South Vietnamese Commissariat for Refugees. COMIGAL it was called, an acronym deriving from the French name for the government agency.

"He's expecting a shipment of medical supplies via the Philippines sometime this week," I said. "We'll be driving out to deliver it."

"Wait a minute. You're leaving the city?"

"The village is only about an hour away. Buck promised I'd be back in time for dinner."

Jakub took a sip of his cocktail. "I don't understand this sudden enthusiasm of yours to go tearing around the Vietnamese countryside, doling out American aid," he said carefully.

"It's something to do. While you're working—" Really, it was more than that. I liked feeling that I was making a difference. People needed the supplies we were distributing, the medicine especially. Infections quickly turned septic in the tropical heat.

"*Najdroższa,* I'd be glad to leave tomorrow, if you're worried about being bored. We're only here because you wanted to be with your brother. Speaking of whom, I wonder where he is."

"At the movies."

Returning from the office, I'd bumped into Gray in the lobby. Freshly shaven and wearing clean clothes, he still looked bedraggled. The Continental wasn't air-conditioned, and his new room faced west. Even with the shutters closed, the afternoon sun turned it into an oven.

"I'm going to catch the five o'clock show at the Majestic. Want to come along?" The Majestic Hotel wasn't air-conditioned either, but its cinema was.

"What's playing?"

"*The Cimarron Kid.*"

"You're kidding, right?" After being awakened in the middle of the night by Audie Murphy shooting off a pistol in the room below, I'd have thought the last thing he wanted to do was to watch the actor on a horse, wielding a rifle. "It's not even a good Western," I protested.

Gray shrugged. "I intend to sleep through it."

"Pleasant dreams."

We'd agreed to meet back at the Continental for a sundowner—an expression he'd picked up in Britain and took every opportunity to use—but the sun had gone down long ago and the movie had to be over. He must have been bushed.

"We could leave him a message," I suggested. "Tell him to meet us at the Rainbow."

My husband lifted my hand to his mouth and kissed my fingertips, one by one. "I have a better idea."

"Does it involve room service?"

"Eventually."

Alone in our room, with the ceiling fan turning and the light from the street lamps along rue Catinat sifting through the slats of the louvered shutters, we undressed swiftly and stood naked, pausing as if to catch our breath before losing ourselves in one another. Jakub moved to close the distance between us, but I held out an arm to stop him. I wasn't done admiring him, the thick, dark hair he wore somewhat longer than was the fashion. It was curlier here, on account of the humidity, and I imagined grabbing it, to anchor myself against that lithe chest, the strong arms pulling me tight as we found our rhythm. I wanted him, but on my own terms. I wanted to arouse him without letting him so much as kiss me in return, relenting only when neither of us could endure it a moment longer.

"Stand still," I said, walking around to admire him from the back. Then I led him to bed. Afterwards, as we lay side by side, our skin cooled by the air wafting off the ceiling fan, Jakub reached for my hand.

"Is it independence you're after, *najdroższa*?"

Was it, I wondered, and would that be such a bad thing, if I were? My husband seemed to think so: five months into our marriage and already I was looking for an escape. He was attempting to be fair-minded, but that's how he saw it, and I could tell he was hurt. How could I explain my satisfaction at the prospect of having work of my own here in Vietnam, useful work? I propped myself up on a bolster so I could look at him while I tried to put into words my desire to do something meaningful, even if only for a short time.

"How old were you when you joined the Resistance?"

"Nineteen. Why do you ask?"

"When I was nineteen, I was living in a flat in London with my older brother, pretending to be sophisticated. I hardly thought of anyone, other than myself. You, on the other hand, were risking your life to save a country that wasn't even your own."

"I didn't have a choice, *najdroższa*."

He did, though. He could have kept his head down, taken the false passport he'd been given and lived a quiet life somewhere as Claude Lassegue. Others did, and nobody blamed them, but he wasn't made that way. Jakub was the bravest, most selfless person I'd ever met—and I knew him well enough to know how embarrassed he'd be if I pointed it out.

I tried another tack. "What about Laurence? She had a choice. I can't imagine it was easy for a girl like her to take up a life of secrecy and hiding."

"Mouche?" He smiled. "She was better suited for it than most of the men I knew."

"How so?" I thought maybe she'd grown up in a family of Communists and developed a second sense for trouble, along with a ready-made network of comrades who could be relied upon to provide her with a hiding place when things got hot.

My husband hesitated, as if he were trying to decide how much to tell me, and how much to hold back. I braced myself for the worst, sure they had been wartime lovers and fearing a confession that he loved her still. Was he on the verge of asking me to let him go, so they could resume their affair in Saigon?

"They caught her," he said. "The Gestapo managed to infiltrate her unit. They were watching from the esplanade of the Place du Trocadéro when she arrived in the gardens for an early-morning rendezvous. Her contact was late—they'd already picked him up—and she knew something was wrong, but being out in the open at that hour, when the park was deserted, there was nowhere to hide. She made it as far as the sidewalk outside the entrance before they apprehended her, and she didn't go down without a fight."

"What happened?" My heart was in my mouth.

"She punched one of them and tried to run away, but they shot her in the stomach—are you sure you want to hear this?"

I nodded, too caught up in Laurence's plight to speak.

"They let her suffer. She was under armed guard in one of the hospitals the Germans had commandeered. They'd removed the bullet and cleaned the wound, but gave her nothing for the pain. Imagine her suffering! They were hoping she'd talk if it went on long enough, but she didn't. Not then, and not in Fresnes prison. Grown men betrayed their comrades after ten minutes in that place. She was a girl from a good bourgeois family, fresh out of lycée, yet she withstood over a year of torture. And Fresnes wasn't the end of it. When they saw they'd get nothing out of her, they sent her to Ravensbrück."

"Ravensbrück!" I'd heard stories about the women's concentration camp in northern Germany. The female guards were reputed to be the cruelest in the entire system, which is already saying a lot. Disease, malnutrition, and exposure claimed many lives, as in all the camps, but prisoners in the infirmary at Ravensbrück were killed by lethal injection, or used as subjects in medical experiments.

The grim expression on Jakub's face confirmed the truth of these stories. "I don't know how she survived, but you saw her. She's back in the fray, reporting on the war, jumping out of airplanes. Without a doubt, she is the most astonishing woman I've ever known."

I said nothing. Of course I'd let him go.

"*Najdroższa*, you're not jealous, are you?" Shrewdly he answered his own question. "So that's what's behind this whim of yours."

"Whim!" I felt as if I'd been slapped. Angrily, I pulled myself away and got out of bed.

"Oh, come here." Jakub opened his arms. "I don't want Mouche, you silly girl. I want you."

*Silly girl.* Fighting tears, I locked myself in the bathroom. Was that all I was to him? I drew myself a bath, the splash of water flowing into the tub masking the sound of my crying. Never before had the gap between my husband's past and my own felt insurmountable, but now I realized the kind of woman he truly wanted, and I was so far from that ideal. How long before he grew tired of me and wandered off in search of someone more like Laurence?

Immersing myself in the tepid water—we never took hot baths in Saigon—I thought back to our first encounter, when the actress I was traveling with abandoned me in a remote town in Southern Italy to go off on a religious quest. I'd assumed it was accidental, our meeting when we did, but subsequently learned that Jakub had taken it upon himself to babysit me until she returned. From the beginning, I was a child in his eyes.

"Cara." My husband was knocking on the door. "Please come out and have something to eat. I've had a tray sent up."

Sooner or later I'd have to face him. Besides, the bathwater was no longer refreshing. I was growing cold. And hungry. I got out of the tub, wrapped a towel around myself, and went out to the bedroom, to find Jakub crouched by the balcony door, talking to a spot on the wall.

*"Jeszcze tylko trochę, przyjacielu. Powoli, delikatnie. Nie chcesz, żeby mucha cię zobaczyła."*

Drawing closer, I observed that the object of his attention was a lizard. The creature was crawling diagonally upwards, toward a fly that had landed in a patch of shadow farther along the wall. It stood twitching, grooming itself, unaware of the predator moving stealthily toward it. The next thing we knew, the lizard had launched itself at the fly and managed to get most of the insect into its mouth.

*"Bravissimo! Co za dzielna mała jaszczurka!"* said my husband, praising the creature in two languages at once. We watched it chew its meal.

Moments earlier I was contemplating the abyss. Now I allowed myself to be led, laughing, to the table in the corner of the room. Jakub pulled a bottle of French champagne out of an ice bucket and popped the cork. He filled our two glasses and kept them filled. We were soon pleasantly inebriated, giggling at one another as we ate croque monsieurs with our fingers (room service had neglected to provide silverware). The crème caramel posed more of a challenge. Already the custard was runny on the plate, melting into the pool of caramel sauce, but we agreed that it would be a shame to waste it. I had a cat in London, Fog, who adored custard. Leaning forward, I slid the plate closer and began to lick delicately at the custard, as she would have done.

"Try some." I pushed the plate in my husband's direction. He seemed dubious of my feline technique, but soon got the hang of it. We took turns until it was gone. Then, chins sticky with caramel sauce and drowsy from the champagne, we fell into bed.

The next morning, we both had headaches. Jakub wasn't wanted on the production until the afternoon, but I was expected at the office at eight. I swallowed two aspirin and brought two to him in bed, replacing the bottle in my purse. I'd have a quick cup of coffee at Givral.

"See you later." I threw him a kiss from the doorway. Always the gentleman, he'd offered to have breakfast with me downstairs, but I told him I'd be happier thinking of him luxuriating in bed. He seemed to have come to terms with my working for Buck. With weekends off, I would only be employed for a total of fifteen days, and not all of them would be spent traveling to remote villages.

I arrived at the office to find Buck in a lather. The aid shipment from the Philippines was delayed in Customs and nobody could tell him when it would be cleared for delivery. This was not the first hitch he'd encountered. Bureaucratic tangles were the rule in Vietnam, not the exception, but the missionary couple were friends of his and he felt badly for letting them down.

"I promised the Laidlaws I'd have those supplies for them by Friday. Stewart's been an awfully good sport, making do with Dooley's leftovers."

"Tom Dooley?" I perked up at the name. Tom Dooley was the Navy doctor who'd headed up the rescue mission that brought North Vietnamese Catholics to the South. "Do you know him, Mr. Polk?"

Buck was pleased that I'd asked. "I had the privilege of meeting Tom at our naval base in Japan in '55. He was on his way home and, let me tell you, that operation he ran was no cakewalk. He looked like hell. Reading his book, you have no idea what it cost him, personally, going in and out of Red Vietnam."

"I didn't know he wrote a book," I said.

"Miss Walden, where have you been? *Deliver Us From Evil* has been a best-seller for close to a year. They even excerpted it in *Reader's Digest*."

"I guess I've been out of touch."

"No wonder, traveling around the way you do, looking for trouble. Cannes Film Festival one day, Budapest the next. Who'd have time for reading?"

It was more than a little disconcerting, how much the government knew about my past exploits, and I didn't understand why Buck kept bringing them up. Was he trying to impress me with the extent of his insider's knowledge? That seemed awfully adolescent, not to mention imprudent. Spies were supposed to be tight-lipped.

"Look," he said, "I'm going down to the wharf to see if there's any way to expedite this shipment through Customs. Why don't you finish unpacking?" He indicated the crates and boxes in the storeroom. "Put away what you can and I'll deal with the rest when I get back."

I set to work, emptying the contents of the containers onto the floor and sorting them by purpose and location. Office supplies (typing paper, ribbons, carbons, a stapler, scissors) went in my desk, forms and folders went into the filing cabinet in Buck's office. Items intended for the missionaries (English-language textbooks, Bibles, pencils) along with odds and ends of questionable value to anyone remained in the storeroom. To this last category I consigned the decks of playing cards and boxes of cigars I found in a carton marked "Training." Was Buck planning to teach the refugees poker? I couldn't see the missionaries approving of gambling, but that might explain why the carton had never been opened.

Unpacking was hot, dirty work. Buck had shown me the second-floor lavatory the day before. It required a key, which we'd hung on a hook in the storeroom. I retrieved it and went down the hall to get myself cleaned up. I was pleased with how much I'd accomplished. Whomever Buck hired to take my place would walk into an orderly situation. She'd also have company, lucky girl. All of the offices on the second floor would soon be occupied by various American-funded Vietnamese enterprises; the building, Buck predicted, would be a hive of activity.

I would have liked having people around to talk to while I waited for my employer to return from the Customs bureau. My watch said it was still shy of noon, but with nothing left to unpack and put away, it seemed like a good time to take my lunch break. I left him a note, telling him where I'd gone and when I'd be back, locked up, and strolled over to the Ben Thanh Market for a bite to eat.

Jakub and I had explored the indoor market over the weekend. Wandering the crowded aisles, we'd picked up some cotton shirts for him. Between the humidity and the unexpected rain showers, it was good to have spares on hand, and the prices were ridiculously cheap, particularly if you could bargain in French. Something we'd both noticed, not only in the market, but throughout the city, was that merchants selling identical wares would be clustered together, enabling you to play them off against one another. Far from resenting this, they seemed to invite it, vying good-naturedly to undercut their fellows. I was used to shopping in Paris's open-air markets, where the competition was less cutthroat. There it paid to be loyal to a few select vendors; regular customers got better service, the choicest cuts of meat, the first fresh mushrooms of the season set aside for you. Here you were everyone's favorite customer until the moment you paid for your merchandise. After that they forgot you.

The food stalls were arranged along the front of the market and down one alley. I looked for the busiest ones, figuring that local people knew who made the best food. Most popular were the stalls selling noodle soups, but the idea of slurping a bowl of pho standing up made me nervous. Instead, I found a woman who was cooking a kind of pancake on a griddle with little half-circle cups. First she poured in the batter, sprinkling it with herbs and scallions. As the cakes fried, their edges turned crispy brown. Just before the batter solidified in the center, she placed a small shrimp on the top of each cup, flipping the cake shrimp-side-down to cook it through. I watched the vendor spoon white sauce over the pancakes and arrange them on a plate next to some lettuce. Customers would wrap a pancake in a leaf of lettuce as if it were a crepe and consume it in a couple of bites.

I pointed and held up three fingers and soon had pancakes of my own. I couldn't believe how good they were. The pancakes were savory, the shrimp tender, and the white sauce turned out to be coconut-flavored. It required dexterity, to wrap and eat my meal one-handed as I needed the other hand to balance the plate, but I was finished in no time.

Next stop was a café on the outside edge of the market, where I could sit under an awning and sip a Vietnamese iced coffee. I'd taken out my compact and was powdering my nose when I glimpsed a familiar goateed profile reflected in the mirror. Gray was walking along the sidewalk on the opposite side of the street, deep in conversation with a smaller man. I could only see the top of his companion's head, but from the straight black hair I gathered that he was Vietnamese. His English must have been very good because, just before the two of them disappeared from view, I saw my brother laugh. I stood up and craned my neck, hoping to catch sight of them farther down the block, but they were gone, swallowed up by the crowd.

I asked Gray about it that evening over drinks. "Who was that Vietnamese man you were with?" It was just the two of us on the terrace. Jakub had phoned to say he'd been delayed.

"What, in the lobby just now? That was the manager. He wanted to know how I liked my room."

"Not him," I said. "Earlier today I saw you walking down the sidewalk with someone, over by Ben Thanh Market."

My brother actually blushed. "You saw us, did you?"

*Us?* I raised my eyebrows. No further prompting on my part was required; he was dying to talk. Pushing aside his beer, Gray pulled a packet of Player's from his shirt pocket, lit one for himself and one for me and told me everything.

"Tam's a translator. A freelancer, although he's trying to get a regular gig with one of the big news outfits out here. He learned English from the Methodists. He knows the words to all three choruses of 'What a Friend We Have in Jesus,' if you can believe it."

"I didn't know there were three choruses," I said, inhaling on my cigarette.

"Exactly." Gray took a puff of his. "He has a lovely singing voice, by the way."

"He sang for you?"

It wasn't only Christian hymns. Tam loved all things

American: cars, Coca-Cola, chewing gum, and movies. Especially movies. It had gotten him into trouble in Paris. He'd been sent there to cram for university—his mother had high ambitions for him—but instead of studying, he'd spent all his time in the cinema. He liked loners. Jimmy Cagney in *The Public Enemy*, Alan Ladd in *Shane*. In France they changed the title to *L'homme des vallées perdues*. The Man from the Lost Valley. Tam caught it at its Paris premiere and Ladd had attended the screening with a bandaged foot and leaning on a cane, slowing him down long enough for Tam to get the actor's autograph. It was his most cherished possession.

"You could probably get him Murphy's autograph without much difficulty," I teased.

"What kind of fool do you think I am?"

"A fool in love?"

Gray sighed. "Is it that obvious?"

I didn't bother to reply. He had plans for the evening, plans involving Tam. I realized it was too soon to ask to be introduced, but I was eager to meet the man who had captured my brother's heart.

An opportunity presented itself the following day. Buck had succeeded in liberating the aid shipment from the Customs authorities. Forms properly certified and all duties paid, it was waiting in a warehouse at the wharf to be claimed. We'd spent the remainder of Tuesday afternoon phoning around, trying with no success to arrange transport from Saigon to the Catholic settlement in Biên Hòa. None of the relevant officials seemed to be available to authorize the requisitioning of a truck. When I arrived at the office on Wednesday morning, he was talking to somebody about it, but judging from his side of the conversation, negotiations were not going well.

The main door to the suite was closed and I'd let myself into my office. I'd assumed that I'd arrived first, but when I got inside, I saw the American through the connecting door. He was sitting at his desk, holding the phone to his ear, listening intently. I started to close the door, to give him privacy, but he motioned that this would be unnecessary.

"Okay, I understand," he said to the person at the other end of the line. "You'll let me know as soon as one comes available? Thanks."

Buck slumped in his chair, closing his eyes and massaging his temples. I'd noticed him doing this frequently during the frustrating series of calls the previous day, perhaps as a way of keeping the nervous tic in his good eye under control.

"Is there a problem, Mr. Polk?"

"The army's trucks are all being used for a training exercise. COMIGAL can get us a couple of jeeps, but we'll have to drive 'em ourselves. I don't suppose you know how to drive a jeep, do you Miss Walden?"

"Heavens, no!" It was flattering that he thought there was nothing I couldn't do, but having observed the behavior of Vietnamese motorists on the streets of Saigon, I had no desire to get behind the wheel of any vehicle in this country, not even a bicycle.

My employer's face bore a look of utter dejection. "I don't know how we're going to salvage this situation. If we don't pick up those medical supplies today, there won't be much left for the refugees. Vietnam is a very poor country, as I'm sure you've noticed, and a bunch of boxes left unattended in a warehouse is fair game. The longer that shipment sits at the docks, the more likely it'll be pilfered. I saw it in the Philippines. You've got to be absolutely on top of these people."

Jakub would be putting in long days for the rest of the week. Gray, however, had time on his hands and his paramour was looking for work.

"We might ask my brother. He can drive anything. And I know where you can find a Vietnamese translator, if you're interested."

"Miss Walden, where would I be without you?"

# CHAPTER SEVEN

## Biên Hòa
## February 20, 1957

Tam was not at all the person I'd expected. For one thing, he was exactly my age, born in the same month as me, April, and the same year, 1933. Our birthdays were days apart, but of the two of us, he looked younger. So young, in fact, that Buck's first reaction was to ask if he shouldn't be in school.

It wasn't only a matter of his appearance. Tam's enthusiasms were those of an adolescent. He seemed starstruck upon meeting me, an actress, although he'd never heard of the one film I'd starred in. Not that he should have. Funded and produced by an American studio, shot in Sicily with an international cast and directed by an Italian, *Stolen Love* had a convoluted storyline that changed from one day of filming to the next. My lover at the time, a British actor who would go on to become rather famous, nearly walked out in frustration. Thankfully, the film had a limited run and was quickly forgotten, leaving no mark on my career.

Tam didn't care about any of this. He'd recognized the name of the American actor who played my husband in the picture, Donald Denning, and was keen to know more about him. Buck and Gray had gone to get the jeeps. Standing guard over the boxes of aid supplies on the wharf while we awaited their return, Tam peppered me with questions.

"Is it true, that he wrote a postcard to his mother every day?"

"Yes, every single day. And he wrote letters, not postcards."

"What about the ten-inch scar on his forearm? Did he ever talk about how he got it?"

I assumed he was referring to an old war injury. Donald had served with Patton's Seventh Army and played a part in liberating Sicily. At some point he'd been wounded, and that was probably what saved his life because he was still recuperating in Palermo when the bulk of his unit was wiped out in the push to take Messina. But the scar Tam was referring to turned out to be the result of a knife fight that Donald had gotten into on the set of *Black River Canyon*, a serial Western from 1947. The cut had required fourteen stitches and cost Republic Pictures a day of shooting. The story was in all the gossip magazines, Tam told me, but the circumstances of the fight, such as who started it and why, had never come out.

"Sorry, he never mentioned a scar," I said, "but I can tell you a story that didn't make the tabloids, if you'd like to hear it."

"Yes, please."

Donald was a character actor who specialized in Westerns. He generally stayed on the right side of the law, playing sheriffs, marshals, cavalry officers, and the like. In essence, he played himself: not only was he a dutiful son, he was a man of upstanding character, a Boy Scout compared to most actors of his generation, although he did have one significant lapse. During his recuperation in Palermo, he'd become romantically entangled with a prostitute. The only reason he'd agreed to appear in *Stolen Love,* in a role well outside the norm for him (he played an American fat cat with ties to the Mafia), was because it got him back to Sicily. The minute we'd finished shooting, he'd gone off to look for her.

"A prostitute? Really? I hope he found her." Tam was not the least bit troubled by the tarnishing of his hero's reputation, so long as it led to a happy ending.

"He found her and brought her back to the United States and married her," I told him. What I didn't tell him was that the prostitute had a son she'd tried to pass off as Donald's, although the boy was much too young to have been conceived during the war. Tonio was a sweet kid and Donald seemed content to accept the child as his own. In any event, I'd heard that his wife had recently given birth to a daughter.

"What should we talk about next?" said Tam. He felt an obligation to keep me entertained. "How about this: I'll give you a line and you tell me the actor who said it and the movie it's from?"

Movie trivia was not my forté. Even as I was trying to convince him that I was perfectly comfortable with silence, he was getting into character, arranging his face into something resembling a tough guy's sneer, top lip curling over his teeth.

"My, my, my. Such a lot of guns around town and so few brains!"

I smiled despite myself. "Humphrey Bogart in *The Big Sleep.*"

"You got it. How about this one?" He leaned back and put his thumbs through his belt loops, as if he were wearing a holster. "Never apologize, mister," he said laconically, "it's a sign of weakness."

"John Wayne?" He had a knack for impersonations, I'd give him that.

"John Wayne. Very good, but can you name the picture?"

I shook my head, stumped. One John Wayne movie was the same as the next, as far as I was concerned. Gray had even less tolerance for movie trivia and Hollywood gossip than I did and I couldn't help wondering what the two of them talked about, when they weren't in bed. Granted, Tam was exceptionally handsome, his eyes large and deep-set beneath thick brows. Soulful, like the teenage heartthrobs girls swooned over in those days. But I'd thought my brother's taste ran to more rugged sorts of guys.

"Do you really not know?" Tam was disappointed in me. "Here's another line. I'm sure you'll recognize it: 'Pony That Walks, my heart is sad at what I see. Your young men painted for war. Their scalp knives red. The medicine drums talking. It is a bad thing!'"

There was no escape. The sun was baking hot and we were standing under the overhang of the warehouse roof, the only patch of shade on the entire wharf and fast disappearing as the sun moved higher in the sky and the shadows shrunk.

"*She Wore a Yellow Ribbon,*" Buck chimed in out of nowhere. "Wasn't that a fine performance!" Now he took a turn at playing John Wayne. "We must stop this war, Chief Pony That Walks."

Tam crossed his arms, like an Indian chief, and made his voice stern. "Too late, Nathan. Young men do not listen to me. They listen to Big Medicine. Yellow Hair Custer dead. Buffalo come back. Red sun. You will come with me. Hunt buffalo together. Smoke many pipes. We are too old for war."

"Yes, we are too old for war. But old men should stop wars."

The two of them would have been content to trade lines of cowboy dialogue for the remainder of the morning, but I was anxious to get going. Stepping away from the shelter of the building, I shaded my eyes and scanned the wharf for Gray. Together, we might succeed at moving things along.

The American followed my gaze. "Looking for your brother, Miss Walden? You'll find him waiting outside the gates. I just need to get the a-okay from the dock agent before they'll let us bring in the jeeps to load them up. The amount of paperwork in this country," he muttered, "more bureaucratic rigmarole they picked up from the French. And most of it's in Vietnamese."

"I can help you with that, sir," Tam volunteered.

"Thank you." Buck extracted an envelope from the inside pocket of his jacket and pulled out a folded sheaf of pages. "This is the inventory that came with the shipment, and there should be a receipt in there for the import duties I paid. Better put it on top, so we don't get charged twice." He handed the papers to Tam, who unfolded them and began diligently to read through the pile.

"Sir," he said, frowning, "what is this one?" He held up an official-looking document, all in Vietnamese, that had been stamped in several places.

The American barely glanced at it. "Oh, that. It's a copy of the form they made me sign yesterday at Customs. Special circumstances, they said, something to do with the medicines. Since you're here, you might as well read it to me. The fellow's English wasn't very good."

Tam drew himself up to his full height and began to deliver a word-for-word rendition of the document. "We

82

hereby certify that on 19 February, 1956, at 5:30 a.m. at Nha Rong Wharf, Saigon Harbor—"

"Cut to the chase," said Buck.

"Yes, sir. Sorry, sir." Tam perused the form. "It describes an incident that occurred during the unloading of the cargo," he summarized. "Several of the boxes were damaged when a heavy piece of equipment fell on top of them."

"Damaged!" The American was suddenly alarmed. "I don't recall hearing anything about this."

"Why, yes. According to the report, there was broken glass—"

My employer was wearing sunglasses, but standing beside him, I could see his right eye twitching behind the lens. I'd had plenty of time to survey the boxes while Tam and I stood in the lee of the warehouse, making small talk. There were forty-three of them, all the same size, all identically labeled with the crossed hands over a shield insignia that connoted US aid. Forty-three had struck me as an unusual number. I'd have expected them to round to the nearest five. Sure enough, the inventory listed fifty boxes.

"Those bastards!" Buck exclaimed. Then he remembered his manners and apologized for swearing in front of a lady. "I'll bet you anything they cooked up that *incident*."

"Maybe we should try to get them back," I suggested.

The American gave a disgusted sigh. "Too late. The goods will have been sold on the black market by now. Happened all the time in the Philippines. Everybody takes his cut. It's my fault for not having been at the docks to personally supervise the unloading. There'll be hell to pay when they get wind of this back home."

"Leave this to me, sir." Tam marched off to the dock agent's office and disappeared inside the building. He emerged ten minutes later, his arms wrapped around a box bearing the familiar US aid insignia. Six uniformed government workers trailed behind him, each carrying identical boxes. Not a single one of them was damaged.

Buck could not stop talking about it on the drive out. "That boy knows how to get things done in this country. And his English! You could almost mistake him for one of us."

Us and them. The American's world divided so neatly. No wonder he liked Westerns, where you could tell the good guys from the bad guys a mile off, from the color of their hats. But it occurred to me that Tam wanted nothing more than to be mistaken for one of us. Chameleon-like, he adapted himself to suit whichever American he happened to be with. He probably imagined that movie gossip was what actresses talked about, and now that he had Buck's number, there'd be no end of John Wayne movie references, I was sure. Next he'd be singing hymns with the missionaries, assuming Methodists and Catholics sang the same hymns. Between saints days and funerals, I'd witnessed a good number of religious processions in Sicily, but none of them involved singing as far as I could recall.

The Laidlaws had neither the time nor the inclination for singing hymns. The Catholic settlement at Biên Hòa was not a single village, as I'd expected, but a sprawling network of villages, each with its own church and parish priest, all of them Vietnamese. Wooden crosses adorned the dwellings, which were laid out in neat rows, as opposed to the helter-skelter arrangement of the huts in the ordinary villages we'd passed en route. Also, the refugee settlements appeared quite industrious. Migrants were engaged in various construction jobs, digging wells, building homes. Patches of land on the outskirts had been cleared for farming and we saw rice paddies being plowed by water buffalo. Elsewhere they were growing fruit and vegetables, women and children working alongside the men, all of them dressed identically in loose-fitting tops and pants, and wearing conical bamboo hats to shield them from the hot sun.

Stewart and his wife oversaw the entire operation. They had help, of course. American volunteers staffed the health clinic and trained teachers throughout the district. Biên Hòa's proximity to Saigon made it an ideal location for small-scale industry. Stewart showed us the plans he was drawing up for a watch factory, a project Buck was certain he could sell to his investors back home. They invited Tam to come and tour the site where they intended to build the factory. Two tall men in blindingly white shirts, striding confidently into the forest, with the small man between them. Gray and I stayed behind to unpack the supplies.

"Do you think he'll do it?" I asked my brother.

"Do what?"

I opened a box of glass syringes and transferred the contents to a sealed container, which I then replaced on an upper shelf in the clinic's examining room. Mrs. Laidlaw had given us copious instructions on where the various items belonged. Everything needed to be carefully stowed, on account of the moisture.

"Will Tam take the job of managing the watch factory if they offer it to him?"

"God, I hope not!"

The vehemence of his response surprised me. He'd known Tam for less than forty-eight hours and already he was entertaining the possibility of upending his life to stay with him in Vietnam. I was still trying to get a fix on Tam. The way he handled the situation with the missing boxes at the wharf revealed a shrewdness that belied his youthful appearance. No doubt there was more to him than met the eye.

"Ugh!" Gray opened a carton filled entirely with yellowing rolls of cotton gauze. "This stuff looks as if it's been around since the Korean war."

"It probably has been, but we are grateful for it all the same." Mrs. Laidlaw had returned with a pitcher of some kind of pale yellow drink concocted from a citrus fruit called calamansi and crushed sugar cane, one of the crops grown in the settlement. The combination was surprisingly refreshing, the sweetness of the sugar cane balanced with the sour juice, and we both drank thirstily.

"Thank you, this was just what we needed," said Gray. "How do you stand the heat out here?"

"Oh, one gets used to it. Our Lord carried the cross to Calvary." Solidly built, with steel-gray hair and a no-nonsense manner, Mrs. Laidlaw seemed straight out of central casting, so perfectly did she fit the image of a missionary's wife. You could imagine her a century earlier, dressed in long skirts and wearing a bonnet, no less steadfast in her faith. Heat stroke, mosquitos, monsoons, yellow fever: like the self-righteous spinster played by Katharine Hepburn in *The African Queen*, she was determined to rise above any affliction sent by nature.

The more I considered it, the more apt the comparison appeared. Hepburn's character was matched against her polar opposite, the dissolute riverboat captain played by Humphrey Bogart—not that Stewart Laidlaw was given to drink, but he didn't strike me as particularly devout. His idea of ministering to his flock entailed turning them into productive employees. I thought Protestants were the ones who believed in the work ethic, whereas Catholics focused more on good deeds, but the Biên Hòa mission proved otherwise. North Vietnamese migrants wanted to get ahead, according to Stewart, and it was his Christian duty to help them. The watch factory was but the first of many initiatives he had planned. Dale Carnegie couldn't have delivered the gospel of self-improvement any more persuasively.

All of this was anathema to my brother. "I'll bet he's trying to sweet-talk him into going to work for them," said Gray. Buck had invited Tam to ride with him back to Saigon. We were following closely behind their jeep and could observe them deep in conversation. I thought it was just as likely that they were trading lines of dialogue from John Wayne movies and started to relate the story of their exchange on the wharf, but my brother cut me off. "I don't like you working for him either, Cara. He's a boor."

I looked out at the forested expanse of road, dense with afternoon shadows. It would be dark by the time we got back to the city, long past the hour for apéritifs. I should have left a message for Jakub at the front desk. He'd be worrying and would blame Buck for keeping me so late.

"You shouldn't have pushed the Yale connection, if you didn't want him latching on to us," I said. The words came out sounding angrier than I'd intended.

"No need to get shirty about it."

"I just wish you'd give him a chance. He could do a lot for Tam, you know, even if he is a boor." We drove in silence for several miles. I suppose it was the American's openness that brought out my protective instincts, that disarming honesty of his. He seemed to lack a layer of skin, the tough, exterior barrier against the world that most people have developed by the time they reached his age. I couldn't imagine how he'd survived this long, vulnerable as he was.

"I'll tell you what," my brother conceded. "Why don't

we invite him to join us for a drink later on, upstairs at the Rainbow? I'll phone ahead and see if I can reserve one of those round tables, off to the side, so we can actually hear one another over the music."

"You won't subject him to one of your political lectures, will you?" I certainly didn't intend to listen to a lecture, after a full afternoon with Mrs. Laidlaw.

Buck thought it was a splendid idea. He'd been to the Chinese restaurant downstairs, but had yet to venture into the nightclub. He claimed to like jazz, but I think he really liked having company in the evening. He was living in the Bachelor Officers' Quarters at the Brink Hotel, a short walk from the American Club, where he generally went for dinner. The food was cheap; for seventy cents, you could get a complete meal, he told us. Beer was fifteen cents, whiskey was a quarter. There were pool tables, but he didn't play pool. Poker was his game, he said. Did we play? I realized that he'd probably acquired the playing cards and cigars in the expectation of starting up a regular game among his compatriots at the Brink Hotel.

"What else do you do in your spare time, sir?" asked Tam.

"I read Perry Mason." Neither Tam nor Jakub had heard of Perry Mason. "He's a defense attorney who solves crimes," Buck explained. "The stories usually start with a client being accused of a murder he didn't commit. Mason investigates and sometimes he gets himself into trouble. Then there's a trial where he lays out the evidence, proves his client's innocence, and reveals the true culprit."

"You mean they're all the same?" said Jakub dismissively. After a full day on the set, he'd have preferred to stay back at the Continental and order room service and was not in the best of moods.

"Well, the structure's the same, but the plot twists are very inventive."

I'd never read the novels, and only listened to the radio serial with half an ear when I was a kid, to humor Father, but Gray enjoyed the stories. Buck offered to loan him some of the books he'd brought with him to Vietnam and I was pleased when my brother took him up on it.

"Which ones do you have?"

The American started to list them: "*The Case of the Black-Eyed Blonde, The Case of the Grinning Gorilla—*"

"The one where the gorilla is hypnotized? I love that story!"

"That's the one, but don't give it away." He patted Tam on the shoulder. "This young man might want to borrow it, to learn how the legal system works in our country."

"Thank you, sir."

"Miss Walden, you might be interested in the one I'm reading now, *The Case of the Terrified Typist.* It's the only case Perry Mason loses."

"Hey," said my brother. "Now who's giving the plot away?"

"I'm not giving anything away. It says so on the cover," said Buck. "The story involves a temporary secretary who gets mixed up in a murder," he added.

"An implausible plot," my husband muttered. He stood up and reached for my hand. "Let's dance."

The musicians were playing a jaunty version of a Jerome Kern classic, "All the Things You Are." Jakub's trio played it too—it was the first number I sang with them—and we often ended a set with it, but this would be our first time dancing to the song. There were already a dozen couples out on the floor and we took our place among them. Some were Vietnamese women with their paying customers, taxi girls they were called. Fowler met Phuong when she was working as a taxi girl in an establishment very much like the Rainbow.

"*Oh, pardon.*" A paunchy middle-aged Frenchman bumped into us and stepped on my foot. In his arms was a slender blonde in a black cocktail dress who appeared embarrassed by her partner's clumsiness. She'd spun away, trailing a whiff of Chanel N°5, before I recognized her.

"Wasn't that Laurence?" In evening garb, the journalist was utterly transformed. Had she walked into the swankiest Paris nightclub and asked for a table, they would have given her one at the front of the room out of sheer gratitude that a creature so exquisite had chosen to grace their establishment with her presence.

"Laurence?" My husband turned his head, to follow the pair's progress. "I've never seen her dressed like that, but you're right. I wonder who she's dancing with."

There were only a limited number of places where Westerners congregated in Saigon, and the Rainbow was top on the list. I supposed it was only a matter of time before our paths crossed. Ever since Jakub had told me about her ordeal at the hands of the Gestapo, I was in awe of the woman. A heroine to rival Joan of Arc, she seemed to occupy a higher plane than the rest of us ordinary mortals. I wanted to figure out what made her tick.

Laurence had divested herself of her companion and was sitting alone at the bar, nursing a whiskey. It was I who suggested inviting her to join us.

"Thank you, and I excuse myself for deranging you. My partner, he is very good editor, but I fear not so good dancer."

Buck stood up at our approach. I was probably the only one who noticed his right eye twitching as Jakub made the introductions. He seemed agitated, even after we sat down, adopting the boisterous persona he'd assumed when we first met.

"Waiter!" He snapped his fingers at one of the men hurrying by with an order of drinks. "Garçon!" he called, pleased with himself for employing the French term.

Laurence frowned. "He is not a boy," she said.

"What's that, you say?" The American turned to the rest of us. "I can't understand her accent, can you?"

"Garçon means boy," my husband explained. "The waiter is a man."

"Oh, my mistake. I'll just stick to English from now on, how about?" He succeeded in attracting a waiter's attention and ordered a fresh round of drinks for the table. Most of us were having after-dinner drinks, crème de menthe and the like, but Laurence asked for another whiskey. Neat.

"Neat, eh?" said Buck, impressed. He took his with soda. When the drinks arrived, he raised his glass to her. "Here's looking at you, kid."

Tam laughed. "Humphrey Bogart. *Casablanca.*"

"Bingo." The American now raised his glass to Tam, who was drinking Coca-Cola, and met his eyes as their glasses clinked.

"I am sorry?" Laurence looked to Jakub for clarification. "*Qu'est ce qu'ils disent?*"

"*Je n'ai aucune idée.*"

"It's a line of dialogue from a movie—" I started to say, but the American put up a hand to stop me.

"Is she telling us that she's never heard of *Casablanca*? A French person who doesn't know the greatest wartime movie about her own country? Why, they even sing 'The Marseillaise,' her national anthem."

I didn't like the way he kept referring to Laurence in the

third person, as if she weren't sitting directly across the table from him and couldn't understand a word of English. Her English was certainly more proficient than his French. Gray was right. Buck's behavior was boorish.

It got worse.

"You know," the American mused, taking a swallow of his drink, "I've never understood why the French didn't put up more of a fight, instead of opening their borders and letting the Germans waltz right in. Maybe Mademoiselle Beverly could enlighten us."

Laurence looked at him blankly, whether because he'd gotten her name wrong or because she didn't fully understand the question. I hoped it was the latter, as did everyone else at the table, including Tam. He was the first to break the silence. The rest of us were too embarrassed, I think.

"If I may, sir, I would like to remind you that Charles de Gaulle opposed the armistice from the start."

"Oh, we all know that Charles de Gaulle and the Free French saved the day," said Buck. "Lucky thing he had the British behind him, because the Resistance in France wasn't good for much except getting themselves captured."

Laurence got to her feet, nearly knocking over her chair in her fury. "You know nothing about the Resistance!" Gray, who was seated to her left, laid a calming hand on her arm, but she shook it off. Picking up her glass of whiskey, she tossed the contents in the American's face, slung her beaded evening bag over her shoulder, and strode from the room.

# CHAPTER EIGHT

## The Rainbow

Buck took the incident in stride. "I guess I put my foot in it, eh?" Pulling a handkerchief from his pocket, he mopped his face, unfazed by the stares and head shaking of the patrons at nearby tables, his good eye not so much as quivering. It was almost as if he were accustomed to having women heave drinks in his face. I felt sorry for him, although there was no excusing his bashing of the French.

"Perhaps we should call it a night," my husband suggested.

The American sighed. "I suppose we should." We accompanied him down to the street and Tam handed him into a cab, negotiating the fare in advance and giving the driver strict instructions on the route in Vietnamese. He then did the same for Jakub, Gray, and me.

My brother was reluctant to part from his lover. "You're not coming with us?"

"I'm sorry, but I haven't been home in two days. My mother will be worrying about me."

I hadn't realized he still lived with his mother.

Gray wrapped an arm around Tam's shoulder and gave him a kiss. "I'll leave the door unlocked," he said, "in case you change your mind. Room 214, remember."

"How could I forget?"

Alighting at the Continental, we found Laurence drinking

brandy on the terrace. They were no longer serving, but she'd paid for a bottle and persuaded them to leave her a few glasses.

"*Je m'excuse,*" she apologized, pouring us each a drink. "*C'était vraiment dégueulasse.*" It was unclear whose behavior she considered disgusting, hers or Buck's. She didn't strike me as the least bit contrite.

Gray raised his glass. "Cheers."

"*A votre santé.*"

We sipped our brandy and watched the parade of motorbikes circling the square. Every so often, a rider would slow down to proposition one of the prostitutes on the sidewalk, zoom off if he didn't like the price she was asking, only to return a few minutes later with another offer. Transactions in Vietnam were always negotiable, Laurence explained. Haggling was *de rigueur*.

I wondered at this. "But people are so poor, and everything is so cheap here. Why not just give them the price they're asking?"

"*C'est une question d'amour propre.*" Laurence turned to Jakub for help. "*Comment dis-tu cela en anglais?*"

"Self-respect," he suggested. "Dignity?"

"*Dignité. Oui.*"

The dance between buyers and sellers in Vietnam, I learned, whatever the commodity, was finely calibrated to make both parties feel satisfied that they were getting a fair price. Tourists who didn't understand this rule were not simply looked down upon. They were mistrusted.

"If someone can't take care of himself, then he can't take care of you," my brother said. "Is that it?"

"*C'est ça. Et ils ne veulent pas de dons de charité non plus.*"

I'd gotten the gist, but Jakub translated for Gray's benefit:

"She says you're right. And they don't want charity either."

Some people, when they drank, became more fluent in a foreign language. This was true of Gray, who could access a vast storehouse of Hungarian, the language spoken by our father and Gray's mother when he was small. But after a couple of drinks, Laurence lost her ability to speak English. She seemed to understand Gray and me well enough, but she couldn't communicate with us in English. Meanwhile, she grew increasingly voluble in French, speaking so quickly that I was soon left behind.

Jakub, who'd put in a long day interpreting for the crew, did his best to provide a running translation as she chattered on, but even he had difficulty keeping up. She'd come to enjoy whiskey in Scotland, he related, where she'd spent a month at a remote estate up in the highlands studying English (*un peu*) and learning various espionage techniques—how to observe someone without drawing attention to yourself, how to tell if someone is following you, how to send coded messages via radio, how to forge documents—before being parachuted back into France.

"You learned all that too, didn't you?" I asked my husband. He'd once doctored a passport, to help Gray sneak into France, and his sharp instincts had saved us from disaster more than once in Budapest.

"On the job, *najdroższa*. Nobody sent me to Scotland."

Laurence nodded. "*Les communistes n'ont pas fait ça.*"

"No," said Jakub. "The Communists didn't do that." He uttered these words with resignation, or perhaps it was merely fatigue. I made a show of looking at my watch. It was past midnight and Jakub was due on the set at the crack of dawn. They'd be shooting in a garage Hornbeck had found in some out-of-the-way district, a sequence that didn't require Murphy's presence. He was supposed to be back in the saddle by the weekend. The truth about his impromptu trip to Hong Kong had come out: the star had undergone emergency surgery for appendicitis. No wonder it was taking him so long to recuperate.

Laurence consulted her own watch, a slim filigree bracelet studded with sapphires that matched the blue of her eyes. "*Dieu, comme c'est tard. Je dois vous laisser aller au lit.*" She embraced each of us, in turn, and we kissed cheeks, bidding her goodnight with vague promises to meet again.

"You're still working for Buck, aren't you Cara?" My brother had paused at the second-floor landing before turning down the spacious corridor to his room. "I mean, I hope you haven't decided to quit."

This was unexpected. "I thought you didn't want me working for him anymore."

"That makes two of us," said Jakub.

If there were a way of bowing out gracefully, I would have abandoned my secretarial career on the spot. Driving for hours in the heat to remote outposts and fraternizing with missionaries was not at all what I'd had in mind when I signed on as Buck's clerical assistant: Mrs. Laidlaw saw the working of God's will behind our decision to come to Vietnam. She insisted that Gray and I get down on our knees, right there in the clinic, so she could offer up a prayer of thanksgiving. Kneeling beside her on the dirt floor was less like giving praise than doing penance, but I felt as if I deserved it. Pride was a sin, wasn't it?

"No, I'm sticking it out," I said, unrepentant to the bitter end.

Gray clasped his hands fervently to his chest in a fair imitation of Mrs. Laidlaw's devotion. "Thy will be done." On the return trip from Biên Hòa, he told us, the American had indeed offered Tam a job, but as his translator, not as the factory manager. It appeared we'd be working side by side until I left the country, and my brother wanted me to keep an eye on things, to make sure his lover wasn't being exploited.

"I'd give it a week," Jakub remarked as we undressed for bed.

"The job?" I wiggled out of my slip. "He'll do better than that. You should have seen the way he handled the Vietnamese bureaucracy. Really. Buck was completely won over."

My husband smiled, but it was tight-lipped and lasted only an instant. "I saw how he handled Buck," he said.

"Yes, he is overly eager to please, isn't he? But I'm sure he'll relax, as he gets more comfortable." I was happy for my brother. Things seemed to be working out his way after all.

"He appears to be very comfortable," said Jakub, the tight smile still in place. For some reason, he'd taken a dislike to Tam. "But I wasn't referring to the job, *najdroższa*. I was referring to your brother's infatuation. It won't last. He's being hustled."

"Hustled? What are you talking about?"

"You probably didn't notice, since you were on my left, but I was sitting next to Buck. Tam was next to him, then came your brother . . ."

"Yes, yes," I said impatiently. There was room for six at the table. Laurence took the empty chair between Gray and me when she joined us. Why was he so intent on recreating the seating arrangement?

My husband continued as if he hadn't been interrupted. "As I happened to be sitting next to Buck, I couldn't help but observe Tam's hand on his thigh."

I was shocked. And dismayed. Here was Gray, contemplating staying on in Saigon after the production ended to be with his new love—who was in the process of seducing someone else right under his nose. My brother would be devastated when he found out, as he was bound to do eventually. Tam seemed to have no loyalty, and no shame. I thought we should tell Gray immediately. If the affair lasted for much longer than a week and he did decide to remain in Vietnam, we'd be gone and there'd be nobody around to console him.

Jakub wrapped his arms around me and stroked my hair. "I have a feeling he won't believe us."

"You're probably right," I said and sighed. Poor Gray. His love life had been a series of furtive encounters, brief interludes of passion in an otherwise solitary existence. Seeing him with Tam, I realized how much he yearned for the easygoing, day-to-day companionship that a couple like Jakub and I took for granted. He was tasting romance for the first time, and I'd never seen him so happy.

Tam must have made his way to my brother's room at some point in the wee hours of the morning. The two of them were eating breakfast together in the courtyard when I came downstairs, sharing a plate of French pastries from the buffet. Gray looked up at my approach and gave me a bleary smile.

"Good morning," I said, resisting the temptation to ask how he'd slept. It was evident that he hadn't. Not that he minded.

Tam got up and pulled out my chair. "Good morning, Cara. Would you like me to bring you some pastries?" He was halfway to the breakfast buffet before I could answer.

"Don't go overboard. She's watching her weight," Gray called after him.

I glared at him. "What are you talking about? I've lost three pounds since we got here." It was the heat. By the end of the day, I had little appetite.

"Don't be so touchy, Cara. I told him that so he'd go easy. Look at how much he brought me."

"That was all for you?" I laughed. "He really spoils you, doesn't he?"

My brother made a pleased sound in the back of his throat, a purr of contentment. "My cup runneth over," he said.

I had to give Tam credit. He knew how to keep a lover satisfied. Maybe exclusivity didn't matter to Gray, although sharing Tam with the American might be a bridge too far. I hoped they'd be more discreet around the office than they'd been at the Rainbow. Catching them in a clinch was the last thing I wanted.

Fortunately, I saw very little of either of them that day. Buck put me to work turning his handwritten notes on the Biên Hòa expedition into a typed report. He wanted two copies, fresh copies, not carbons: one to keep on file and one to send on to his "investors," as he continued to call his US government overseers. A large aid shipment was due to arrive on Friday, this one destined for an outpost in the Mekong Delta. The American intended to submit the paperwork in advance, hoping to avert the kind of shenanigans we'd encountered with the previous shipment. He was taking Tam with him to the wharf.

"Hold down the fort, Miss Walden!" he called cheerily over his shoulder as the two of them set off.

The first copy of the report took nearly three hours to

complete, but the second went faster since I was working from a typescript, rather than having to decipher my employer's handwriting. I'd finished both by noon but was reluctant to take my lunch break and have Buck return to an empty office. The storage room still required attention, and I set myself the task of organizing the remaining odds and ends, consolidating the stuff into as few boxes as possible, which freed up a good deal of space. Finally, at 2 p.m., I locked up and went across to Ben Thanh market for shrimp pancakes and an iced Vietnamese coffee.

The proprietress greeted me like an old friend. I guess she didn't get many Western customers, particularly not solitary young women. The market was less busy at that hour, and she kept plying me with delicacies, cloyingly sweet pastries made of some kind of bean flavored with fruit like mango or banana, and glutinous rice cakes in pastel hues. I tried a taste of each, to be polite, but since we shared no common language, it was hard to communicate when I'd had enough. When it was time to pay, I remembered Laurence's advice about negotiating and offered her half the amount she was asking. At first she acted angry, but I held firm and we eventually reached a compromise that seemed acceptable. When we parted, she smiled and nodded as if to say that she hoped I'd be back. I'd still probably paid more than I should have.

"Miss Walden, is that you?" the American bellowed as I came down the hall. Rather than bellow back, I quickened my pace, arriving a bit winded at his door. He was seated at his desk, reading a manual of some kind, pages of blurry print bound with brass fasteners between two pieces of cardboard.

I braced myself for a reprimand. "Sorry I'm late, Mr. Polk."

"No need to apologize. You finished the reports and even found time to clean up the storeroom, I see. Very efficient!" Buck got up from behind his desk and ushered me over to the conference table. "Allow me," he said, pulling out my chair. "Cigarette?" He reached for the enamel box that lay in the center of the table, one of our many purchases from Magasins Charner. I'd filled it with Lucky Strikes since the American didn't smoke.

"Thank you." I took one and accepted a light, watching his face for the telltale tic. There it was. Was he trying to get up the courage to fire me? Really, there didn't seem to be enough work to warrant a secretary, no matter how efficient she was. I drew on my cigarette and waited for the inevitable. I'd lasted only marginally longer in this job than as an extra, but I'd be relieved when the job ended.

Buck settled himself across the table from me and cleared his throat. "Er, Miss Walden?" He paused yet again, and I found myself wishing he'd just fire me and get it over with.

"It's okay," I said reassuringly. I thought he was worried I'd make a scene.

His question came out of the blue. "Have you ever been camping, Miss Walden?"

"Camping?" I croaked. I'd inhaled too quickly and was overcome by a fit of coughing.

The American dashed around to my side of the table and pounded me on the back. "Are you okay?" I nodded, standing up and moving away from his over-exuberant efforts at first aid. After a moment, I'd caught my breath and was able to speak.

"Are you talking about camping in a tent? With sleeping bags and flashlights?" Some of my friends at boarding school had been Girl Scouts, but I hadn't spent much time in nature as a kid, unless you counted skinny dipping in Father's pool.

"Camping in a tent, yes. The journey's too long to complete in a day, and the Mekong Delta is swampland, but don't you worry. I've sent young Tam off to acquire everything we need: pup tents, sleeping bags, mosquito netting, and insect repellent. He knows all the markets in Saigon."

"Another of his many talents?" I couldn't resist saying.

"Yes, indeed." Buck's cheeks were flushed, and I doubted it was on account of the heat. He and Tam hadn't devoted the entire time they were gone to filling out paperwork at the wharf. What they did on their own time was their business, but I had no desire to learn whether a pup tent was large enough to accommodate two. The idea of roughing it in a mosquito-infested swamp was unsavory enough.

"Come now, Miss Walden," Buck chided, evidently reading my expression. "Think of it as an adventure! We'll be leaving Monday morning and I promise to have you back to your husband, safe and sound, Tuesday night."

"I'll have to ask him," I said, stalling. I was pretty sure Jakub would veto the idea. In fact, I was counting on it, and my husband didn't let me down. What I hadn't counted on was an assassination attempt on President Diem the very next day.

I'd left work that Friday afternoon secure in the knowledge that Buck and Tam would be making their way to the Cái Sắn resettlement area in the Mekong Delta without me. Jakub, Gray, and I were having sundowners on the Continental's terrace when the American appeared on the sidewalk in front of our table.

"Mind if I join you?" He didn't wait for permission,

flinging himself into the empty chair that Gray had been saving for Tam and ordering a whiskey and soda, which he downed the moment it arrived—this from a man who could spend an entire evening nursing a single beer.

"Is something wrong, Mr. Polk?" His right eye was twitching, if I needed any further evidence of his distress.

Buck signaled for a refill. "They tried to kill the president!"

"Eisenhower?" we all said in unison, stunned.

"No, Diem."

"Who tried to kill him?" said my husband. Instinctively, he wrapped a protective arm around my shoulders.

"The Communists. Who else?" His drink arrived and the American took a long swallow. Then he seemed to decide he'd had enough and pushed the glass away. The president, he told us, was about to make a speech up in the Central Highlands on the government's land redistribution policy, the policy that had resulted in the creation of resettlement areas. He was seated on a dais with his agricultural minister and a couple of local officials when a gunman opened fire on the platform party with a submachine gun. Where else could he have gotten hold of a weapon like that, except from Hanoi?

I nestled myself more snugly against Jakub. "You say he survived?" President Roosevelt died in office when I was a kid. I remember the shock of losing him, with the war still raging. In troubled times, a country needed stable leadership.

"It was pure luck," Buck admitted, reaching once more for his whiskey. "The assailant got off one round before his weapon jammed. He hit the agricultural minister, but Diem escaped without a blemish. I'm told he insisted on going ahead with his speech, once his security forces had subdued the gunman. Cool as a cucumber, he was." The American chuckled. "I'd call this a victory for our side, in the overall scheme of things."

"I'm not sure the agricultural minister would agree," said Jakub. "Or doesn't he count in the overall scheme of things?" His tone was mild, but I sensed his outrage, and I felt the same way. Vietnamese politics wasn't a team sport.

But Buck was oblivious to scorn. "We've got to show the Communists that we're not afraid. Otherwise it's Munich all over again: give 'em an inch, they'll take a mile."

"Are you sure that Munich's the analogy you want?" my brother asked. "Hồ Chí Minh's no Hitler. If you ask me, it's Spain all over again."

"How so?" Despite himself, the American was intrigued.

"The Việt Minh defeated the French with the help of China. You might say that Mao, in funding the Vietnamese, played the part of Stalin. He aided the democratically elected government of Spain against Franco's Nationalists—"

"Now, wait a minute," Buck interrupted. "You've got things mixed up. The Spanish Nationalists were fascists, for one thing. Nazi Germany put their air force at Franco's disposal, and provided weapons and training, along with ground troops. They bombed the hell out of Guernica. Then Mussolini got in on the action."

"Actually, that's my point," said my brother, barely able to disguise his triumph. "Franco wouldn't have won without outside help, as you acknowledge. Meanwhile, the Western democracies sat on their hands and let the massacre happen." As a college student, he'd marched in support of the Spanish Republic and considered joining a battalion of American volunteers to fight the Nationalists, under the auspices of the Communist Party. Father had talked him out of it, but this brief flirtation had been enough to get him blacklisted.

"Munich. Spain." The American pounded his fist on the table, knocking over his glass. Only Jakub's quick reflexes saved it from rolling off the edge and shattering on the pavement. Within seconds, a waiter materialized to clean up the mess, but Buck was too caught up in the argument to notice any of this.

"I'll tell you one thing," he continued belligerently, "we won't make the same mistake again!"

"Would you like another, sir?" the waiter offered.

"What's that? Another whiskey? Yes, I would."

My husband met the waiter's eye and shook his head. "How do you propose to do that?" he asked Buck, aiming to distract him.

"By going ahead with the aid delivery on Monday. You may not like the calculus, Mr. Abramowicz, but the lives of tens of thousands of North Vietnamese refugees are in the balance. The settlers at Cái Sắn are depending on us to deliver that shipment. We can't let them down."

I didn't like the way he kept using the words *we* and *us*, but this was what I'd signed up for, wasn't it? Up until now, the job had been easy. Too easy. Here was a chance to prove myself. If Laurence could march into danger, so could I.

"Go, by all means," said Jakub, throwing cold water on my heroic ambitions. He'd also picked up on the *we* and *us*. "I applaud your fortitude, but leave my wife out of it."

Buck fixed him with a stare and for once the good eye wasn't twitching. "I need your wife's help. And your brother-in-law's. COMIGO—that's the name of the South Vietnamese government's refugee agency, and don't ask me what it stands for—is providing us with trucks and drivers. Why, they're even sending us down with a military escort! The settlers won't know that this is an American operation unless we put an American face on it."

"A military escort," my husband repeated incredulously. "For an aid shipment?"

"Well, it's just a jeep with two soldiers, but they'll be accompanying us for the entire route."

"Will the soldiers be armed?" Buck nodded. "You're expecting trouble, in other words." Jakub's arm was clamped firmly around my shoulders. I wasn't going anywhere.

"Count me in," said my brother. Smitten, he'd go anywhere so long as he could be with Tam.

"Glad to have you on board. You can drive one of the jeeps." Buck shook his hand. He then returned his attention to Jakub. "Look, I'm not denying the risk, but we really have no alternative. There's medicine in the aid shipment. Hundreds of dollars' worth of vaccines that'll spoil if we don't deliver them immediately."

My husband stood, and clearly expected me to follow suit. "Nobody's stopping you."

"Why don't you come with us, Mr. Abramowicz? We could use a man like you," said the American. I had to hand it to him. Shrewdly, he'd hit upon the one way to secure my husband's cooperation. A whiff of danger was no deterrent to Jakub. On the contrary: he liked being in the thick of it and, if the truth be told, I'd be glad to have him along. I trusted him more than two soldiers to keep me safe.

Monday morning found me seated beside Buck in a jeep, clinging for dear life to the windshield as we attempted to catch up with our military escort. Jakub was following us on a motorcycle, with Gray and Tam's jeep not far behind him. Every so often, when we hit a smooth patch of road, I'd risk letting go of the windshield with one hand to turn around and make sure they were still with us. The Vietnamese soldiers in the lead vehicle cared little about such niceties, bumping along the highway (a term I used loosely), taking the curves at velocities we dared not match. The four cargo trucks carrying the supplies had long ago disappeared from view, but their drivers were local men who presumably knew the route. This was Buck's first visit and, having no map—the resettlement project was so new, the surveyors had not yet made one—we were dependent on our escort to show us the way.

I reassured myself that Cái Sắn couldn't be too hard to find, even without an escort. The project was huge, dwarfing the one at Biên Hòa. In barely a year, COMIGO had overseen the construction of some two hundred villages along the canals that fed into the Mekong River. The US government provided financial and technical support, delegating the administration of aid to religious organizations. I'd made the mistake, earlier in the drive, of referring to the shipment we were delivering as "charity," but Buck set me straight.

"We're not dealing with a population of indigents looking for a handout, Miss Walden. These migrants are eager to be earning their own living. We aim to give them training and equipment and just enough supplies to help them get on their feet." Cái Sắn was well on the way to self-sufficiency, he told me, its forty thousand settlers—farmers, for the most part, from rural regions in the North—busily dredging canals, clearing fields and removing undergrowth from forests, planting vegetables and bringing long-neglected rice paddies back into cultivation. The project was considered a great success, a model for future collaborations between our two countries. He couldn't wait to see it.

Gray was jealous that Jakub got to drive a motorcycle. It was an old Peugeot, a 1940s classic, beige colored with pre-war styling. "Will you look at that! Girder forks and hand-gear change. And such style! Trust the French to make the rear light look sexy."

Jakub had offered to let him drive it so he and I could travel in the jeep, but my brother had merely contented himself with a short test run while the cargo was being loaded into the trucks. He hadn't liked the idea of Buck and Tam riding together. Simple possessiveness, or was he picking up on the sexual undercurrents between them?

"There they are, up ahead. About time they—" The American's relief at having caught up with our escort was palpable, but short-lived. Lost in my own thoughts, it didn't dawn on me immediately, as we drew level with the soldiers' jeep, why they'd stopped, and what had happened to them when they did.

A mass of jungle vegetation blocked the road in front of us. Palm fronds, stalks of bamboo, leafy plants with their roots exposed, as if they'd been torn out of the ground and flung randomly on top of the heap, formed an insurmountable barrier. The soldiers had been ambushed and shot. They were both dead.

# CHAPTER NINE

## En Route to Cái Sắn
## February 25, 1957

"Oh, Jesus." Buck shifted into reverse, giving me a panoramic view of the carnage as he backed around. He whipped the steering wheel with so much vigor that he knocked his sunglasses right off his face. "Don't look!" he shouted, accelerating away from the scene.

Too late. There was no way of unseeing the horror I'd witnessed, although I was having difficulty making sense of it all. Where was the driver's head? Surely it wasn't that pulpy mess on top of his shoulders. The door to the passenger's side of the jeep was open and the other soldier's body hung at a bizarre angle, half in, half out of the vehicle, one hand still grasping the door handle. A living man could not have held himself in that position, but I was confused by the blood flowing from his mouth, as if he were vomiting.

Jakub roared up alongside us on his motorcycle, motioning with the palm of his hand for me to get down. Whoever shot the soldiers might still be out there. We had to get away now! Gray and Tam had already turned around and were zooming down the road ahead of us. My husband kept apace with our vehicle. He was using his body to shield me.

Obediently, I scrunched lower until my back was practically flat against the seat, legs stretched as far forward as they could go, grateful for modesty's sake that I'd chosen to wear slacks on this expedition. Despite the heat, Buck wore a blazer and was perspiring heavily, the sweat stain beneath his armpit approaching the proportions of Lake Michigan. I turned my head upwards to watch the treetops speeding by overhead. If anything happened to Jakub, it would be my fault. I'd brought us here, to the edge of disaster, and for what? Because I was bored. If we made it out, I vowed to become a better person, a woman worthy of the man I'd married.

*If we made it out.* I tried to distract myself from the danger we were in by conjuring up the movie I'd watched on Saturday with Gray and Tam. *Shane* was probably my brother's favorite Western. We'd seen it together when it opened in London in the fall of 1954 and while I wasn't keen to see it again, Jakub was working and there was much to be said for spending the hottest part of the day in air-conditioned comfort.

The matinee was packed with Americans, rowdy young men for the most part. Who knew there were so many of them in Saigon? I'd felt their eyes on me as the three of us took our seats—I was virtually the only female in the movie theater—but my brother's presence sufficed to keep them in line, and I suspected that my presence made it easier for him to be with his lover in public. Vietnam may have been more accepting of homosexual liaisons, but it had seemed prudent for me to sit between the two of them in that gathering.

Afterwards, seeking privacy, we went back to Gray's room at the Continental to talk about the picture. Second time through, *Shane* had grown on me, but I'd have liked an unambiguously happy ending.

"Why did he have to leave?" I asked. The lonely outsider who comes in to save the town and rides off into the sunset was an old formula, I knew, but Shane didn't have an Indian sidekick for company.

Gray gave me one of his older-brother looks. "You weren't listening, were you, Cara?"

"Yes I was," I insisted, hearing the little-sister whine in my voice.

"Then you should remember what Shane told Joey."

I searched my memory, but all I could recall was the kid calling mournfully after Shane to come back. "What did he say?"

"I know, I know!" said Tam, eager as a schoolboy. He was sitting on the floor by Gray, leaning against my brother's legs.

"Well, go ahead then."

"A man has to be what he is, Joey. Can't break the mold."

Gray tapped him on the shoulder. "My turn," he said. "Joey, there's no living with a killing. There's no going back from one. Right or wrong, it's a brand. A brand sticks."

"Now you run on home to your mother," Tam chimed in, "and tell her . . ."

". . .tell her everything's all right and there aren't any more guns in the valley," the two of them finished in tandem. My brother was over the moon. Who was I to tell him that Tam had used the same ploy with Buck? No doubt there were others; he must have practiced, to make it come out so smoothly. Of all the young men looking for a diversion in the Majestic that afternoon, surely a few would have been susceptible to Tam's charms. He

111

probably trawled the place on a regular basis and Gray was just one of the many fish he'd caught in his net. How long would it take before my brother realized it?

I brought the conversation back to the ending of *Shane*. "So, he's leaving because he's a killer and they're peace-loving citizens?"

"That's right." Gray nodded sagely. "They'll always remember him as a hero, back there in the valley, but his kind is obsolete and he knows it."

At this, Tam looked up. "Obsolete?"

"Well, yes. What do they want with a gunfighter, now that they're rid of the villains trying to drive them off their land?"

"There are always more villains," Tam said.

Idly, my brother played with a silky strand of his lover's hair. "And not enough gunfighters, eh?"

"Miss Walden." Buck was slowing down. "We're safe now, Miss Walden. You can sit up again."

Carefully, I straightened up. There, by the side of the road, were the four trucks. The Vietnamese drivers were clustered together on the berm, having a smoke, oblivious to the danger ahead. We pulled over and Buck got out and crossed to their side of the highway, beckoning for Tam to come along and translate. I got out too. Jakub had parked a bit farther ahead and was removing his helmet and goggles as I approached.

"*Najdroższa.*" The instant he saw me, my beloved gathered me in his arms and held me tight. I struggled not to cry. I didn't want his sympathy. I accepted full responsibility for getting us into this mess, I just didn't know how to get out of it.

Neither did Gray. He'd joined us and I could see that he was also looking to Jakub for a solution. The three of us passed around a canteen of water while we strained to overhear the American's conversation with the drivers against the sound of the idling of the one of the trucks' engines. It was a refrigerated truck carrying vaccines, and Buck was insisting loudly that an alternate route to Cái Sắn must be found, lest this valuable cargo spoil.

"Tell them we'll pay them extra," we heard him say. Tam conveyed the offer. "What's that? Speak up!"

Tam raised his voice. "Do you have dollars, sir? They won't do it for piastres."

"I have plenty of dollars, but they don't get paid until we get there and they've unloaded every last box of American aid. Tell them that."

One of the men pantomimed holding the money, running his thumb along the tips of his fingers. Buck extracted his wallet from his trouser pocket and drew out some bills. He gave one to each driver—as a good faith gesture I assumed—replacing the rest in the wallet, which he returned to his pocket. Then he removed his jacket, giving them (and us) ample time to observe the black leather shoulder holster he wore strapped to his chest.

"I didn't know he was packing a pistol," said Gray.

My husband was frowning. "Neither did I."

They both looked to me for confirmation that the American didn't always carry a concealed weapon on his body. I had to think for a moment because, while he tended to work around the office in shirtsleeves, he might have stashed a gun in a desk drawer or somewhere close at hand. Outside of the office, he generally wore a jacket, I told them. The day we visited the department store. The night at the Rainbow. Biên Hòa was an exception. He'd had his jacket on when we were at the docks, but he'd removed it at some point on the journey. I distinctly remembered Buck and Stewart Laidlaw in their white shirts with the sleeves rolled up, the day we visited the missionary settlement.

"Yes," agreed my brother, "I remember that too."

It surprised me that he'd noticed. His attention that day had been focused exclusively on Tam, as I recalled, his yearning so strong I'd felt it coming off him like heat.

Jakub was pursuing his own train of thought. "He must have felt comfortable in that settlement."

*As opposed to here.* With a sinking heart, I completed the sentence in my head. We weren't out of the woods yet. The only reason for showing his gun to the drivers was to warn them to watch their step.

"It wasn't a coincidence, was it," I asked my husband, "all of them stopping back here, just short of the ambush?"

"I don't believe in coincidences."

I was struck by the hardness of his voice. My beloved was trembling with fury. Instinctively, I reached for his hand, to ground him, and was reassured when he clasped my fingers in his own. But the moment Buck and Tam concluded their negotiations with the drivers, he released me and strode across the road to meet them. His hands, I noticed, were now clenched into fists.

Gray gripped my arm to prevent me from running after him. "Let him go, Cara." My brother knew me too well. As a child, I used to try and get between my parents when they were arguing. I hated confrontations of any kind and would do anything in my power to prevent one. Seeing Jakub enraged was truly frightening, he was ordinarily so calm, and the knowledge that it was all on my account, because I might have died in the ambush that killed the soldiers, did not comfort me in the least. We shouldn't have been here in the first place. Buck owed me an explanation and I ought to be the one to press him, not Jakub. Pulling away from

Gray's restraining grasp, I followed Jakub across the road, leaving my brother no choice but to trail along behind me.

The American hailed us with a hearty wave. "All set! Young Tam tells me we're less than an hour from Cái Sắn. Isn't that right?"

"Yes, sir. The men have an old French map that shows the back roads. There appears to be a short cut."

"Humph! Might have told us sooner," Buck grumbled. "Ah, well. Never mind." He patted Tam on the rump. "On your way, young fellow. You'll be with me for the next leg. Miss Walden, you can ride with your brother, unless he'd prefer to take the motorcycle?"

"My wife is going with me," said Jakub coldly. "I'm driving her back to Saigon this very minute."

Buck was taken aback by this defection, but he recovered quickly. "Don't be foolish. You'll never make it there by nightfall. Trust me: you'll be far safer within the settlement than out in the open."

"We'll take our chances." Jakub turned his back on the American and addressed himself to Gray. "Coming?"

My brother was watching the retreating figure of his lover as he crossed the road and made for the jeeps. "I'm not sure I want to be traveling after dark, especially not on a motorcycle."

"We can stop in that city we passed on the way here, Cần Thơ. Find a hotel or a guest house. We don't have to camp outdoors." This last sentence, although directed at Gray, was said for Buck's benefit. I snuck a glance at his face. Without his sunglasses to hide it, his right eye was twitching madly.

"You can't abandon me now!" he protested. "It's vital that we deliver this food and medicine to the refugees."

Jakub was having none of it. "You expect us to continue

with these men as our guides?" He inclined his head in the direction of the drivers. "How do you know they didn't have a hand in planning the ambush?"

"It's possible," Buck admitted. "There've been reports of unrest in this region over the past couple of months. Scattered incidents. Diem's people being harassed, that sort of thing. No American has been the targets of an attack; it was Vietnamese attacking one another. After the assassination attempt last week, it seemed prudent to have an armed escort, but I thought the presence of armed soldiers would be more than enough to deter the insurgents."

"Reports of unrest! Insurgents!" Now it was my turn to be outraged. "You didn't mention any of this when you invited me to join this—what was the word you used? Oh, yes. Adventure."

The American hung his head. "Forgive me, Miss Walden. I didn't want to worry you unnecessarily. This entire area used to be a Việt Minh stronghold. Most of the population moved away during the war. That's what made it such prime territory for resettling the refugees. The land's been fallow for years."

"Moved away?" said Gray. "As if they chose to leave?" He crossed his arms and glared at Buck. "Fled, more likely."

"*Nettoyage*," murmured Jakub.

"House cleaning?" I wasn't sure I'd heard him correctly.

"It's a euphemism, *najdroższa*. French army slang for clearing out the population of a village they suspect of harboring terrorists. They're still at it in Algeria. You know that."

"Yes." It upset me to think about it. Torture, rape, kidnappings. There was no hiding from it in Paris. The newspapers were full of atrocity stories about the war, the French ones and even *The New York Herald Tribune*, which I bought at the newsstand near our apartment every morning. A campaign of terror was being waged in Algeria and was beginning to spill over into the streets of Paris. Neither side was pure; both employed violence in the name of their cause, and more often than not, innocent people were the targets of that violence. I hadn't realized it was the same here. Maybe it was the same everywhere, I thought bleakly, remembering the violence we'd seen in Hungary. People my age, their future ahead of them, cut down like wheat.

Gray wasn't ready to let the American off the hook. "Wouldn't it be more accurate to say that the villagers were driven out as part of a concerted policy by the French army?"

"Well, it's a bit more complicated," Buck explained. "After the war, it was sort of like the wild, wild West down here. Lawless. The Lower Mekong Delta used to belong to Cambodia, you know, and there are large numbers of Khmer throughout this area, along with other tribal peoples. The Vietnamese considered them savages and treated them accordingly. Can you blame the Khmer for retaliating when they got the chance? The French couldn't have prevented the killing, but they ought to have stopped it sooner."

"Why didn't they?" I asked.

"Because it served their interests, letting their colonial subjects murder one another?" Jakub suggested. He was not ordinarily so cynical.

My brother agreed wholeheartedly. "Divide and conquer. Standard operating procedure for imperialists since Roman times, at least."

"Look," said Buck, "I'm not going to defend the French, but don't you see? That's why we're here. America has a moral obligation to help this country! Did you know there was a famine up north in '45, following the Japanese occupation? Close to a million died! A Marshall Plan for Vietnam would have made all the difference, but instead we abandoned them. Is it any wonder they turned to Hồ Chí Minh? Poor suckers had no option but to throw in their lot with the Communists. Now's our chance to make up for it."

I was almost swayed by this little speech, and I saw Gray nodding his head, but my husband was not persuaded in the least.

"A missed opportunity, certainly. One of countless mistakes made by the Western democracies after the war."

The American gave him a shrewd look. "I forgot, you're Polish."

"I was thinking about Hungary, actually."

"Oh, yes. The three of you were eyewitnesses to the tragic events in Budapest, weren't you?"

"Tragic events." Jakub gave the words a bitter edge. "Why is it," he pressed, "that we're always looking in the wrong direction when the Communists move in?"

"I'm afraid we'll have to save that discussion for another day," said Buck. "We've got a shipment to deliver. "

My husband didn't budge. "You haven't been listening. We're not going with you. It's too risky."

"Damn right it is." My brother appeared to have made up his mind to join us. "For all we know, those drivers are in cahoots with the guys who ambushed us. They could be somewhere nearby, waiting to finish the job. You think you're going to defend us with one little pistol?"

The American winked with his good eye. "Ah, but I have

more than this one little pistol." He lowered his voice. "I imagine you gentlemen know how to shoot." Jakub and Gray said nothing, but Buck took their silence for assent.

"What about you, Miss Walden? Ever handled a weapon?"

"Sorry." Was there nothing he thought I couldn't do? In fact, we'd been taught to fire a rifle at the Wentworth Academy, but I was a lousy shot.

Jakub was staring at Buck in disbelief. "How many guns did you bring?"

"More than enough for our purposes."

"Are you telling us you've got an arsenal back there?" My husband jerked his head in the direction of the trucks. Suddenly I saw the point of this expedition: the American's insistence on having me come along to normalize the mission, the Vietnamese government's loan of trucks and drivers, the precaution of bringing along a pair of armed soldiers. This was no ordinary aid delivery, although it was meant to look that way. We were arming the settlements against the insurgents.

"Hey! What's going on?" Buck shaded his eyes with a hand and peered across the road. "Is that young Tam, fighting with one of the drivers?"

"Where?" demanded my brother.

No sooner had the American pointed to the motorcycle than Gray took off running. The driver, however, a much burlier figure, had the upper hand, and before my brother could reach them, he'd knocked Tam to the ground and mounted the machine. We heard the sound of the engine revving up. Suddenly, he'd turned and the bike was coming straight at us. I screamed. Jakub was yanking me toward the undergrowth as Buck drew his pistol and fired at the man's chest. A patch of blood blossomed on his white shirt

119

as he swerved, barely missing the other drivers. The swerve became a skid and then the bike went down.

The American didn't wait to find out whether his first shot had been fatal. "Get her out of here!" he barked at Jakub over his shoulder as he went to finish the job. We heard the sound of the second shot as we were crossing the road.

My brother was kneeling in the dirt by his lover, who was clearly in agony. "He's badly hurt. I don't know what to do to help him." Gray was beside himself.

"Let me take a look at him," said Jakub, kneeling on Tam's other side. Gently, he traced along Tam's ribcage with his fingertips, pressing and releasing, inching his way down the chest. "Breathe," he instructed. "That's good. And again." He moved his fingers across to the right armpit.

Tam yelped.

"That's the spot." He unbuttoned Tam's shirt and, sure enough, a lurid bruise spread upwards from Tam's armpit to just below his right shoulder. My husband studied the injury for a long moment.

"Did he break a rib?" Gray wanted to know.

"Hard to tell. He seems to be breathing okay, so if it is broken, I don't think it's pierced a lung. But I'm no doctor. We need to get him someplace where he can be properly looked after."

That meant continuing the journey to Cái Sắn with the American.

We set off for the resettlement area in a new configuration. Buck drove the refrigerated truck, keeping closely behind the Vietnamese driver who seemed most familiar with the territory. He was followed by another truck, then came Gray and Tam's jeep, behind it the final two trucks, with Jakub and me bringing up the rear. The motorcycle was too damaged to drive. We scuttled it, along with the driver's corpse, in the undergrowth by the side of the road. I told myself I'd think about it later; getting upset was a luxury I couldn't afford just then.

Tam was feeling no pain, thanks to the morphine we'd unearthed among the boxes of medicines. There were less than a dozen vials—Buck suspected the rest of the consignment had been "lost in transit" and would soon be turning up on the black market—enough for the difficult trip through the jungle and the drive back to Saigon if carefully husbanded. The American had administered the drug himself, tapping the syringe to release any air bubbles, then pinching the skin of Tam's upper arm and slowly injecting the narcotic. I tried not to speculate about where he'd gained such expertise and when else he'd had the occasion to use it. Gone was the fraternity boy with his bumbling bonhomie. The new Buck had succeeded in impressing upon the remaining drivers that he was utterly ruthless. The men were scared of him and, I must admit, so was I, although I tried not to let it show. For once my acting skills served me well.

"Miss Walden, I'm going to teach you how to fire a gun," he'd said as we waited for the drug to take effect. He'd handed Jakub the pistol while he was tending to Tam. Now he took out the bullets and handed it to me. "Stand with your feet slightly apart. Bend your knees a little. That's right." He explained how to aim by focusing on the gun sights, aligning the top of the front sight so that it ran through the center of the target. I remembered this much from school. I even remembered which was my dominant eye (the left one, although I was right-handed), that it helped to use two hands to steady yourself, and that you were supposed to look at the gun, not the target.

Buck raised my right arm until it was straight out and moved the left one to rest at an angle below it, adjusted my fingers so they were positioned below the trigger guard— all except for the index finger, of course, which he told me to press against the bottom outside the guard until I was ready to fire. He positioned my body so I was facing the dead driver and his downed motorcycle, which I found disquieting, to say the least.

"You want to use the fleshy pad on your index finger, not the tip," he advised. "And you don't pull so much as squeeze the trigger. Try it a few times, just to get the feel of the mechanism. Aim at the torso. Then we'll let you practice with real ammunition."

He expected me to shoot at the body of the dead driver! I lowered my arm and turned my back on the corpse.

"Come now," the American chided. "This is no time to be squeamish, Miss Walden. The whole point of this exercise is to teach you how to defend yourself. You've got to be able to kill a man. A dead enemy is as good a place as any to begin."

Killing an assailant was one thing. If someone I loved were threatened, I was pretty sure I could pull the trigger. I'd once lunged at a man who was threatening Jakub with a dueling pistol, a man I'd known all my life. I hadn't stopped to think, I'd just sunk my teeth into his forearm until he dropped his weapon. But it seemed wrong to pump bullets into a human body, just for target practice. Disrespectful. I handed back the gun.

Buck's eye was twitching furiously. "He was Việt Minh. Do you know what those animals did to the bodies of their opponents? They disemboweled them and left the entrails—"

"That will be quite enough," said Jakub, coming over and putting an arm around me. I thought he meant to draw me away, putting an end to the callous exercise, but that wasn't his intention. "Give her something else to shoot at," he told Buck.

"Excuse me, sir," piped up Tam behind us. The morphine must have kicked in. He'd gotten to his feet and was leaning against Gray, the pair of them flanked by the three remaining drivers. I'd been concentrating so hard on my aim that I hadn't noticed when they crossed to our side of the road, but the American must have known they were close by. Was the purpose of having me use the dead driver for target practice to harden me, or to intimidate them?

Tam made another attempt to get his attention. "They say we should leave, sir. It gets dark fast in the jungle."

"We'll leave when I'm ready to leave."

Buck went to the rear of his jeep, rummaged around beneath the tarp covering the camping equipment and our overnight things, and extracted a tan leather suitcase. Inside were several pistols and boxes of ammunition, which he distributed to my husband and brother, keeping one of each for himself. He instructed Jakub to take the remainder of the stash back to the jeep and keep watch over them. Then he placed the empty suitcase in the middle of the road, repositioning me to face it, loaded the bullets into the pistol and put it in my hand.

"Fire when ready!"

I will admit, he was an excellent instructor. I shot two rounds, reloading the gun myself, and the majority of my shots hit the target. If called upon, I would know what to do.

The sun was setting as we got underway. Almost immediately, we turned off the main road onto a dirt track that ran parallel to a canal. It felt as if we'd entered a terrarium, the foliage was so thick and so diverse, every tree colonized by other plants: ferns, vines, orchids. In some places the bamboo had taken over, suffocating the surrounding vegetation and making the route so narrow I was surprised the trucks could make it, but they plowed straight through, leaving a trail of broken stalks in their wake. I hoped the narcotic was still doing its job, because the jolting got worse the farther we ventured into the jungle, and I worried about Tam's ability to withstand it.

Abruptly, we swerved left, heading into a glade of some sort and leaving the canal behind. Monkeys screamed from the trees and I caught a glimpse of a black snake slithering across the road. I half expected to see Johnny Weissmuller come swinging into the scene in his Tarzan costume. As a kid, I was used to seeing Father's guests lounge *au naturel* around the pool, so the sight of a muscular man clad in a skimpy loincloth was nothing special.

Ahead of us, the trucks were shifting into a lower gear. "It looks as if we've arrived at the village," my husband said, peering ahead through the dusty windshield.

"Where?" In the fading light, all I could see were a cluster of thatched bamboo huts on stilts arranged haphazardly around a larger rectangular building constructed of wood. We really had no choice but to stop because the road ended at the huts, although it felt very wrong to me. If this was our destination, it was far more primitive than the settlement at Biên Hòa, and there wasn't a cross in sight. Had the drivers led us into a trap? Instinctively, I reached for the pistol in my handbag as we braked behind the others.

Jakub motioned for me to put it away. A crowd of villagers

had materialized in the dusk and were closing in on the convoy. They weren't Christians. They weren't Vietnamese. They were tribal people, men and women of all ages and a good number of children, most of them naked from the waist up. My thoughts about Tarzan weren't so farfetched, although none of these people was the least bit muscular.

"Smile, *najdroższa*," said my husband, coming around to open my door. "We want them to know we're friendly." Hand in hand and beaming for all we were worth, we walked forward to meet them.

# CHAPTER TEN

## Ta Philippe

An elderly figure leaning on a staff separated himself from the group as we approached and stepped forward. He wore a loincloth like the other males, but his torso was covered by a woven tunic and he was wearing socks and shoes, although the latter had seen better days.

"*Vous êtes . . . Américains?*" he asked, the slight pause in his question, combined with his peculiar inflection on the final syllable of the word "Americans," conveying not uncertainty regarding our nationality, but disdain for our culture. I'd taken him to be a member of the tribe, his skin was so tanned, his face so wrinkled you couldn't tell the shape of his eyes, but he was as French as they came. Never mind the native garb. His bearing was that of an aristocrat, someone with a "de" in front of his name, an apartment in one of the better districts of Paris, and a crumbling mansion in the countryside.

I knew his ilk; the trio had a regular gig in one of the ritzy clubs in the sixth arrondissement. We performed in formal attire, tuxedos for the musicians, an evening gown and elbow-length white gloves for me. The same staid repertoire, week after week, two sets with no room for improvisation. Jakub said there was no joy in playing that way, but the club paid twice as much as the seedy joints in the Latin Quarter and the gig occasionally led to even more lucrative bookings at private functions where he and the fellows could cut loose.

"Ta Philippe!" A child was pulling on the hem of the old Frenchman's tunic and pointing to the head of the convoy. I glimpsed Gray and Buck making their way through the crowd, supporting Tam between them. My brother's lover looked absolutely miserable. With every step, he winced. The ride must have been sheer hell.

"*Qu'est-il arrivé? Qui est ce jeune homme?*" The hauteur vanished as my husband explained who we were and the circumstances that had brought us to the village. Our interlocutor spoke to the men around him in their language, directing them to carry Tam into one of the huts. Gracious now, he invited us to stay the night and rest, after our ordeal. He personally would attend to our friend's injury. Although he was not a doctor, he had picked up a good deal of jungle medicine during his time living among the Khmer Krom.

"Khmer Krom?" I repeated. "*Qu'est-ce que ça veut dire?*" The beauty of conversing with an aristocrat was that he spoke proper French, not slang, and carefully enunciated every single syllable. Having learned the language out of a textbook, I understood him perfectly and was even emboldened to ask questions. If only Parisians were more like him, I'd have been at home in the language.

I had to wait for an answer until after Tam was settled in a hammock, a poultice applied to his chest and another dose of morphine enabling him finally to doze off into oblivion. Ta Philippe—the word "ta" meant grandfather in Khmer, and Philippe was his first name—had offered everyone in the convoy hospitality for the night, but Buck and the drivers had been eager to be off. Now, having eaten a simple meal of fish steamed in banana leaves and coconut rice prepared

by the village women, we sat on mats in our host's hut and
sipped tea by the light of an oil lamp.

"Cigarette?" offered my husband, proffering a carton of
Gitanes.

Ta Philippe accepted one with pleasure and waited for
Jakub to light it before he spoke. "Khmer Krom," or "Khmer
from down below," referred to ethnic Cambodians living in
the Mekong Delta, he told us. "*Ils s'appellent eux-mêmes
Khmer Krom.*" This was the name they gave themselves;
the Vietnamese called them "Moi" (savages), and he was
ashamed to admit that he'd employed that derogatory term
when he first arrived in the village, some thirty years earlier.
The French had picked it up without realizing that it was an
insult.

"Didn't know, or didn't care?" Gray wondered aloud.

Ta Philippe looked to Jakub for a translation.

"*Il veut savoir s'ils ne savaient pas ou si ils s'en fichaient,*"
my husband said.

Our host shrugged. "*C'est la même chose, n'est-ce pas?*"
It amounts to the same thing, doesn't it?

I remembered what Buck had told us about the bloody
score-settling after the war, how the French had stood by
and allowed it to happen. Suddenly the Vietnamese drivers'
impatience made sense. They were afraid of the Khmer
Krom—afraid enough to take their chances traveling
through the jungle after dark rather than risk being murdered
in their beds by their enemies. But how had this Frenchman
managed to gain the tribal peoples' trust, despite getting off
on the wrong foot? It would have been rude to ask outright,
but gradually I managed to put the pieces together.

Philippe Marie Guillaume de Rosset was the second son
of an old noble family from central France. He'd attended
the prestigious Lycée Louis-le-Grand and was studying

anthropology at the equally prestigious École normale when his studies were interrupted by the First World War. Unlike his older brother and many of his classmates, Philippe survived the conflict, but the war changed him. As a junior officer, he'd felt cut off from ordinary soldiers, envying their easy camaraderie, so different from the rivalries at school. His brother's death at Verdun meant that he would inherit the title of duke, upon his father's passing, but the prospect of overseeing the family estate and producing an heir of his own did not interest him. Instead, he took a job as an ethnographer with a team going out to Cochinchina (as the southern third of Vietnam was called) to catalogue Khmer Krom beliefs and traditions. The project was expected to last two years, but Philippe stayed on after the other researchers left. He'd fallen in love with a woman from the village and they had three sons.

"*L'un d'eux devrait hériter de mon titre, je suppose, et de la terre qui l'accompagne.*" One of them ought to inherit my title, I suppose, and the land that goes with it. His wife had very much wanted to see his home, he told us, but Philippe kept putting off the trip. First he argued the children were too small to make such a long sea voyage. Then came the Second World War, which made travel impossible. In any event, he believed they were safer in the village. The Vichy authorities left them alone, as did the Japanese. There were no roads into the swamps in those days and the Khmer Krom, having no association with the French, were not viewed by the occupiers as a threat. But after the war the Việt Minh took advantage of the chaos in the region to eliminate all vestiges of colonialism, including even a benign presence such as an aging anthropologist whose sympathies, if the truth be told, resided with the cause of independence.

They came for him one night, but the villagers repulsed

the attackers. Ta Philippe thought it would be safer for his family if he wasn't around. When the Communists came again, the villagers hid him, so they murdered Philippe's wife—in front of his children no less.

I gasped. *"C'est affreux!"*

Ta Philippe acknowledged my shock by bowing his head. *"J'aurais dû les ramener tous en France,"* he said quietly. I should have brought them all back to France. It was on the tip of my tongue, to ask him why he hadn't left then. The Việt Minh had evidently remained active in the region. Wasn't he still a target, he along with his sons and their families?

Our host seemed to divine my thoughts. *"Mes fils méprisent les français."* His sons despised the French, and with good reason. Perhaps we did not know that the Michelin company and other colonial enterprises employed the Khmer as indentured laborers on rubber plantations throughout the Mekong Delta. Conditions were appalling: one in three succumbed to disease or overwork, he told us, or returned crippled, the ethnographer's detached persona in full display. The overseers used whips, and those deemed dangerous were sent to the notorious Poulo Condore prison on Côn Sơn Island, where inmates were literally worked to death. No, he said without a trace of self-pity, his fate was tied to the village. He would be laid to rest here, his soul joining the unquiet spirit of his murdered wife.

What could any of us say? Lying with Jakub that night in our sleeping bags under our tent of mosquito netting, we sought comfort in one another's bodies, subsuming the ache of Ta Philippe's loss in soft kisses and gentle caresses. I couldn't imagine how you went on, after a tragedy like that, a tragedy for which you blamed yourself. Jakub had endured the deaths of his entire family back in Poland and a part of him, I knew, wished he'd died back there with them. Tenderly, we made love and when he came, shuddering inside me, I held him as tightly as I could, afraid he might break with the release of all that sorrow.

Buck returned early the next morning in a jeep truck. In place of the Vietnamese drivers, he'd assembled a crew of clean-cut American college boys, volunteers with the resettlement project eager for a furlough in civilized Saigon.

"Let me help you, ma'am." A freckled fellow handed me up into the back of the truck, which was laid with bedding for Tam, a corner kept free for me to tend him during the ride. I knew Gray would have preferred to stay with his lover; he'd slept on the floor of the hut where they'd put him and although he reported that Tam had not been too restless during the night, there would be no avoiding the jolts during the first leg of the trip as we wended our way out to the main highway. Ta Philippe had wanted to keep him in the village for a spell, to give him time to heal. He'd invited the three of us to stay as well, and my husband was ready to take him up on the invitation. Jakub had little interest in continuing his work with the production team and I certainly wasn't going to be working for Buck any longer. Why not make the best of things and use the opportunity to learn more about the Khmer Krom and the anthropologist's work with them?

It was Buck who insisted that Tam needed to be examined by a proper physician. "He needs . . . *il a besoin* . . .how do you say X-ray?"

Jakub finished his sentence. "*Notre ami a besoin d'une*

*radiographie pour pouvoir déterminer la gravité de ses blessures.*"

"*Une radiographie. Je comprends.*" Ta Philippe shrugged and wished us safe travels, the cold aristocrat once more. I felt badly for insulting him by not trusting him to care for our friend, but the American had a point. We'd been pumping Tam full of morphine and our supply was nearly gone. He might improve on his own, as the anthropologist seemed to believe—the fact that he'd made it through the night without needing another dose suggested that rest would do the trick—but we didn't really know the extent of his injuries. The closest clinic was in the Cái Săn resettlement area, and it was pretty rudimentary. What if Tam's condition got worse? I knew we couldn't afford to take the risk, but I hated leaving Ta Philippe with the impression that all Americans were the same, that we were all like Buck.

As it turned out, Tam was in such agony by the end of the five-hour journey that Buck and the college boys took us straight to the hospital. To the American's credit, he didn't cut corners. Hôpital Grall was the best medical facility in Saigon, and that's where we went. Founded as a military hospital at the time of the French conquest in the mid-nineteenth century, it was expanded to serve French residents in the colony and still possessed a turn-of-the-century grandeur. Driving through the iron gates was like entering a park, shady lanes giving onto formal gardens filled with fragrant blossoms. Recuperating patients might sit out on the wooden porches that ran the length of each of the hospital buildings, breathing in the scented air and imagining that they were not sick, but on vacation. True, the place was staffed by nuns. The Sisters of Saint-Paul de Chartres wore the starched white cornette of the traditional nursing orders, their sharp creases showing no sign of wilting in the sultry afternoon heat.

The Sisters themselves were more accommodating. We must have looked a sight, having traveled for two days in open jeeps on dusty roads, sleeping in our clothes. While Tam was being X-rayed and examined, we were given clean towels and shown the washrooms. The ladies' washroom was well-stocked with creams and lotions, including a bottle of pricey eau de toilette that I applied liberally. Refreshed, and smelling of lavender, I returned to the waiting room to find Jakub and Gray sipping coffee from porcelain demitasse cups. The nuns had even provided a basket of sliced bread and wedges of Laughing Cow cheese. We were all feeling human again by the time Tam hobbled out, supported by a nun on either side. Our friend had fractured two ribs, but there was no indication of a punctured lung or any other complications. The doctor had bandaged him up and wanted to see him again in a week. Until then, he was to rest and avoid strenuous activity.

"Are you comfortable?" asked Gray as he helped Tam get settled in the front seat of a Citröen deux chevaux, the most spacious vehicle available from the taxi company we'd called. Tam assured him he'd be fine riding in the back, but my brother was concerned that one of us might jostle him inadvertently. Traffic was heavy in the city, even on weekday evenings.

Tam and his mother lived in one of Saigon's outlying districts, but Lily owned an antique shop in the commercial center, two blocks beyond the Central Post Office and Notre-Dame Basilica and only a mile from the Continental. She was open seven days a week, hoping to attract the tourist trade. The plan was for all of us to go there, then send the two of them back to their apartment in the cab and walk the mile to our hotel. Since Lily had no phone, there'd been no way of alerting her about Tam's injuries and he was apprehensive about her reaction. She didn't know he'd gone down to the Mekong Delta, he confessed, and would be furious when she heard about the attack on the convoy. Tam was all she had, and she tended to be overly protective.

"Where did she think you were?" I couldn't help being curious about their relationship. I'd been left pretty much to my own devices as a kid. Nobody paid attention when I didn't come home at night. Father had barely batted an eye when I got pregnant at seventeen, but then, Vivien had conceived me at the same age. Tam's mother was equally lackadaisical, it seemed.

"With you," he responded without a trace of embarrassment. "She knows that I have a new *friend*."

"Does she?" said Gray, pleased.

"My mother doesn't miss much."

This proved to be an understatement. The three of us had gone into the shop, leaving Tam to wait in the taxi. We'd had to park a good ways down the block, and when we walked in, she thought we were customers.

"*Bonsoir. Comment puis-je vous aider? Cherchez-vous quelque chose en particulier?*"

Petite, her delicate beauty set off by a pale yellow silk *ao dai* embroidered with butterflies, Lily seemed the quintessential Asian woman, submissive and ultra-feminine, but the moment my husband explained who we were and why we'd come, the demure facade vanished. Peremptorily, she instructed us to mind the shop while she rushed out to see her son. When she returned, her manner was brusque. After counting the money in the till of her cash register (did she think we might have stolen some?), she pulled down the shutters and took one last look around the shop before ushering us outside so she could finish locking up. Then she set off toward the taxi with crisp, short steps, her movement barely hampered by the close-fitting garment she wore. We weren't sure whether we were supposed to follow her.

"*Venez, venez!*" she urged, over her shoulder, addressing us as if we were a pack of unruly children. "*Dites au revoir à mon fils.*" Come along and say goodbye to my son. Obediently, we trailed her down the sidewalk.

"Whew," said my brother under his breath. "What a dragon lady! Tam wasn't kidding."

Lily waited, a trifle impatiently, while Jakub and I shook hands with Tam through the cab window. When it was his turn, Gray reached in to place a hand on his lover's cheek, gazing longingly into his eyes.

"When can I see you?"

Tam spoke to his mother in Vietnamese, his tone wheedling but persistent. The two of them went back and forth for several minutes until he succeeded in wearing her down. Drawing a slip of paper and a pen from her purse, Lily jotted down their address and thrust it into my brother's hand.

"*Vous pouvez venir nous voir demain matin,*" she said grudgingly. You may come and see us tomorrow morning.

# CHAPTER ELEVEN

## Phú Nhuận District
## February 27, 1957

Lily's invitation may have been intended for Gray alone, but my brother asked Jakub and me to come with him for support. Early the next morning, we all piled into a taxi and drove to the apartment in Phú Nhuận District, a fifteen-minute trip. Once Lily left for work, we were free to leave as well.

"You kept your cool when the convoy was attacked by Việt Minh terrorists and now you're afraid of a tiny woman?" said Jakub grumpily. He'd have preferred to spend the Monday morning lolling in bed. It was actually raining, for the first time since we'd arrived in Saigon, the scent of jasmine wafting in from the pots on our balcony. I was again out of a job, and Jakub had the week off while Hornbeck and Mankiewicz frantically screened the second set of rushes from the production. This batch had been delayed, owing to strikes at Air France, and when it finally arrived, some of the scenes were missing. Either they'd have to do without or reshoot the entire sequence at Cinecittà. Time was running short, and all energies were now focused on the big disaster scene to be staged in the square in front of the Continental. Jakub had agreed to help out on the set, but he wasn't needed until Sunday. Four entire days to spend together, doing as we pleased!

Tam and his mother lived in a narrow building on a street crowded with coffee stalls and food vendors, bicycles and scooters parked helter-skelter on every available inch of sidewalk. They occupied the top two floors, which might sound lavish, but each floor was essentially a single room, a kitchen and living area down below and a bedroom and bathroom above. Lily slept upstairs, while Tam slept in an alcove curtained off from the *salon*, as Lily called it, a room furnished in Western style, with a sofa and an armchair, a table tucked against one wall opposite a breakfront crowded with knickknacks. The topmost shelf held a small, household altar containing a framed photograph of a Vietnamese man, a vase of fresh flowers, and a bowl of dragon fruit. Three sticks of incense burned in a glass cylinder, perfuming the air with sandalwood.

Lily was dressed traditionally, as before, this time in a pale pink *ao dai*. She wore her hair loose, giving her a girlish appearance. But while her manner was less forbidding, she lacked warmth.

"I welcome you to my home," she said, her smile as impersonal as an airline hostess's. She led us to the sofa. "You sit yourselves and I make coffee. You like a *café vietnamien* or a coffee *americain*?

"Please sit down," Tam corrected from his corner.

Lily repeated the phrase, mimicking him perfectly. "Please sit down."

"*Maintenant, vous pouvez leur offrir du café,*" he said schoolmarmishly. Now you may offer them coffee.

"You like—"

"*Would* you like."

"Would you like a *café vietnamien—*"

"Vietnamese coffee."

"Would you like a Vietnamese coffee or a American coffee?"

"*An* American coffee."

I couldn't bear to listen to Lily struggle any longer and answered her hastily in French. "*Café vietnamien, s'il vous plaît.*"

"*Vous parlez très bien français!*" she said, her voice suddenly animated. You speak French very well.

In fact, I'd done little more than repeat her question, followed by the word "please," but observing the effect of this small gesture upon Lily, I responded to her compliment with the polite textbook formula. "*Vous croyez?*" Do you think so?

Tam glared at us from his sick bed.

"My son, he is helping me learn English for . . ." Lily paused, searching for a phrase, which despite her best efforts, continued to elude her. "*Comment dit-on 'les clients américains' en anglais?*"

"American customers?" suggested Jakub. "*Vous souhaitez que plus de clients américains fréquentent votre magasin d'antiquités.*"

She nodded vigorously. "*C'est ça. Il y a très peu de français à Saigon ces jours-ci.*"

"Speak English, *Maman,*" Tam scolded. The reprimand, although addressed to his mother, was obviously meant for Jakub and me as well, and I felt stung. Who was this imperious person? I understood that with the exodus of the French, Lily needed to learn English so she could get more American customers into her shop, but browbeating her in front of guests wasn't the right way to go about teaching her. I was embarrassed on her behalf.

"*Puis-je vous aider à faire le café?*" Pointedly I offered, in French, to help with the coffee, earning a smile of gratitude.

Lily set a kettle on the stove and reached for the coffee grinder. "*Connaissez-vous les grains de café cà phê Chồn?*" She was asking whether I was familiar with the beans they used to make Vietnamese coffee. I was not. Soon I was learning more than I wanted to know about the harvesting process, aided by Jakub, who had joined us in the kitchen area and faithfully translated Lily's account for me, interjecting his own commentary along the way.

Wild civets were fond of the cherry (Cherry? Is that what they call the fruit of the coffee plant?), selecting only the best of the crop and consuming them at peak ripeness. Enzymes inside the animals' stomach then broke down the outer layer of pulp, permitting the bean to ferment (Ah, just like potatoes for vodka!) and removing much of the bitterness. We might have noticed a chocolate taste? (*Najdroższa*, this next part is rather unusual. Try to keep an open mind.) The semi-digested beans were excreted in clumps. Laborers on coffee plantations cruised the grounds, collecting the civet feces. The beans were then rinsed and roasted.

"Wait a minute," I said, disgusted. "That chocolaty taste you mentioned: that's civet droppings?"

Lily must have been able to tell from the expression on my face that I'd grasped the essential feature of Vietnamese coffee. Laughing, she assured me that roasting sterilized the beans. "*Ne t'inquiète pas. La torréfaction stérilise les grains de café.*" I was glad that she'd switched from the formal to the familiar form of address. I liked her better than I liked Tam and could see that Jakub shared my partiality. Really, who could blame her for being prickly when we'd shown up out of the blue, three strangers, with her injured son in tow? She hadn't even known he'd left Saigon. Now, however, liberated from his demand that she speak English, she seemed eager to make up for her coldness of the previous day, covering the table with a fine linen cloth, upon which she placed a tray of sliced pineapple. From a cabinet in the breakfront she pulled a set of four blue and white porcelain teacups rimmed with silver, antiques from the looks of them and quite exquisite.

"*Que c'est beau!*" my husband exclaimed. The cups were indeed beautiful, each hand-painted with a landscape of pine trees curving against a background of mountains, half shrouded in clouds. Maybe it had to do with the milky morning light, or was it a feature of the glaze that lent the trees a delicate shimmer, as if their boughs were encased in ice? A glass forest whose beauty resided in its fragility.

Lily bade us sit, summoning Gray from Tam's bedside. As she busied herself pouring coffee and serving us slices of pineapple, she related the cups' history. This style of Chinese ceramics, with its pale wash of cobalt blue and distinctive silver rims, was known as Bleu de Hué, she explained. They'd been made toward the end of the nineteenth century in Jingdezhen, the porcelain capital of China, for the imperial court of Thành Thái in Hué.

"*C'est vrai?*" my brother asked in evident disbelief, although he was too polite to challenge her account outright. Father collected antiques—Walden Lodge was full of valuable objects d'art—and he'd taught us both to be skeptical of dealers' claims regarding the history of items they were trying to sell. Every piece of furniture once belonged to someone famous, every tapestry had hung in a French château, according to the so-called experts, but I thought Lily made a convincing case for the teacups' royal provenance.

"*Je vous assure que ces tasses appartenaient à*

*l'empereur,*" she insisted. Turning one upside down, she showed us the reign mark on the bottom. All ceramics made for the Nguyen dynasty carried the name of the emperor who commissioned them. What's more, she said, we could tell from the design painted on the cups that they were used by Thành Thái's concubines because each member of the royal household had a different motif: dragons for the emperors; phoenixes for his wives; lotuses for the queen mother; unicorns, birds and flowers for the princes; crabs and ducks for pottery used in the kitchen. She couldn't remember which motif was designated for the emperor's daughters, but landscapes belonged to the concubines.

I recalled the nearly windowless dwelling in the Imperial City our guide had pointed out to us. Was it not cruel, I asked our hostess, to remind the emperor's concubines of the outside world by giving them china cups decorated with outdoor scenes?

"*Il ne faut pas supposer qu'ils étaient malheureux.*" One mustn't assume that they were unhappy. Lily herself had been the mistress of a French army officer, she told us frankly, a *chef de bataillon* stationed in Vietnam with a wife and children in Paris, to whom he'd returned after the French withdrew from Vietnam. She had no regrets over their eight-year affair; Guillaume had been very good to her, setting her up in the antique shop and paying for Tam's schooling at the elite Lycée Pétrus Ký in Saigon. He was like a second father to her son, she told us. He'd even pulled strings to get Tam into a private prep school in Paris.

Tam disputed this last statement. "He didn't do it for me, *Maman,*" he said from his bed in the corner. "You both wanted me out of Saigon."

Lily turned to Jakub for a translation. "*Qu'est-ce qu'il a dit?*" My husband hesitated, not wanting to be caught in the middle of a family dispute, and Lily sensed his discomfort. "*Je m'excuse,*" she said, apologizing for putting him on the spot. She turned and spoke sharply to her son in Vietnamese, and was answered in the same language and in the same tone. The exchange grew heated. They seemed to have forgotten the three of us were in the room. Jakub raised an eyebrow and glanced at his watch, telegraphing his desire to leave.

"*Il faut partir,*" I announced to the room at large. We must be going. At this, Tam directed another torrent of abuse in Vietnamese toward his mother, who made no effort to refute him. Cowed, she collected our cups and carried them over to the sink, motioning for us to wait while she washed and dried them. From the breakfront she extracted a shoebox. Carefully, she wrapped each cup in tissue paper, nestling them inside one another and filling the empty space around them with crumpled newspaper. Then she handed the box to me.

"Oh, no," I said, refusing the gift. "It's too much. We couldn't possibly—" I looked to my husband to communicate this more delicately in French.

"*Nous sommes sensibles à ta gentillesse, mais nous ne pourrions pas accepter un cadeau aussi précieux.*"

Lily spoke rapidly to her son in Vietnamese, who responded without rancor. It was she, this time, who seemed to have the upper hand.

"My mother is grateful to you for bringing me home safely and begs you to take the cups," Tam said, his English stilted, as if he were a hostage reading from a prepared script. "In the Buddhist tradition, the gift giver is more blessed than the recipient."

What could we say? Carrying the shoebox, Jakub and I said goodbye to Gray and Tam and thanked Lily for the gift and for her hospitality. She'd invited us to share a cab with her back to the city center, but we'd demurred, preferring to make our own way on foot. We were in no hurry. The rain had stopped and we had no place in particular to go.

"Didn't you say that Tam was educated by Christian missionaries?" my husband asked, taking my arm and steering me around a beggar on the sidewalk. He was surprised by the shrine on the breakfront, and by Tam's easy elaboration of Buddhist teachings.

I told him that I didn't think much of the Methodists' teaching had rubbed off on Tam, apart from the hymns. The Vietnamese, in any event, seemed to find no contradiction in worshiping the Christian God while carrying on with their own traditions. In the Catholic settlement of Biên Hòa, I'd noticed an altar in the common dining room much like the one in Lily's apartment. Community members left offerings to appease their ancestors' spirits, particularly during the Tet holiday. Mrs. Laidlaw admitted they'd had no success at stamping out the practice, but they'd come up with a compromise, installing a statuette of the Virgin Mary among the flowers, fruit, sweets, and Buddhist trinkets. Whenever she or her husband passed by the altar, they made a point of crossing themselves, and the habit soon caught on. The next step was to consecrate the shrine at the Nativity feast.

Jakub nodded. "It has always worked that way." Pagan sites would be rededicated to one of the saints by the early Church and, after a generation or two, these ancient holy places had become Christian. He'd once visited a church in Bologna built on top of a temple to the Egyptian goddess Isis. Over the centuries, there'd been several additions to the original sanctuary—Santo Stefano, as the church was named, was actually a cluster of seven churches—but in the oldest building, you could still see a stone slab that appeared to have been used for human sacrifices. It now served as an altar.

I shivered involuntarily "Are you trying to scare me?"

"Not at all." He stopped walking, put down the box, and took me into his arms. "The Sette Chiese are quite magnificent. We could go to Bologna if you like."

"Do you mean it?" I said, kissing his nose, his chin, his Adam's apple. We hadn't had a proper honeymoon. A week after our marriage in September, we were in Paris, where the trio played six nights a week. A month later we'd gone to Hungary with Gray, barely escaping before the Soviet tanks rolled back in. Now this little jaunt to Vietnam had turned into a nightmare. I'd be relieved when we were on the plane to Rome and could put the whole thing behind us.

My husband laughed and kissed me back. "Why not? From Rome we can catch a train to anywhere in Italy. Florence, Venice, the Amalfi coast. There are so many places I want to show you, *najdroższa.*"

How had I gotten so lucky?

Our walk through Tam and Lily's neighborhood had brought us to a canal, its banks lined with tin-roofed shanties, many on the verge of collapse. At one time the waterway may have been used for transportation, but today it was clogged with garbage. Hundreds of people were living in squalor, half-naked children played by the water's edge, and the stench of raw sewage was so powerful, my first inclination was to turn away, but Jakub urged me onwards and as we continued to walk, I was able to see past the ugliness, collecting impressions about the lives of the people we observed. The old man, his toothless smile as he held his grandson in his lap while the child's mother fed the boy spoonfuls of pap. Women gossiping as they rinsed clothes in the filthy water. A group of men playing a game with multicolored dice. The sound of a stringed instrument being played somewhere nearby.

I was thinking that this was the real Vietnam, not the tidy villages where the migrants were being housed. And then, as if I'd summoned him, Stewart Laidlaw appeared out of nowhere, striding purposefully through the busy neighborhood. Instinctively, I moved out of his line of sight, flattening myself against the angle of an open door. The missionary paused in front of a dwelling and spoke to a Vietnamese man who appeared to be guarding the entrance, judging from his crossed arms and wide stance.

"What's he doing here?" said Jakub in a loud whisper.

"Ministering to the poor," I ventured. The two of them disappeared into the shack.

"Mr. Quang?"

He'd recognized the sentry as the local fixer, whom I'd nearly succeeded in putting out of my mind since our run-in some two weeks earlier. Of course, my husband hadn't come on the first aid mission to Biên Hòa. He didn't know who Stewart was until I identified him as Buck's associate. What had brought this incongruous pair to the slums of Phú Nhuận District? Jakub handed the shoebox to me and edged closer to the building, hoping to overhear the conversation within. The shack's walls were paper thin.

I hung back, anxious to be gone. Westerners didn't often venture into this part of Saigon and we were attracting unwelcome attention. Children paused in their games to stare openly at the foreigners, adult conversations foundered, then ceased entirely. I worried that the sudden hush would be perceptible to Mr. Quang and Stewart. What if they came out to investigate?

From inside the shack came a howl of pain. A man could be heard yelling in Vietnamese, his shouts punctuated by

145

thwacking sounds that elicited more agonizing cries from the unseen victim. I saw fear on the faces of the people around me. Mothers dragged their children away. The dice players took their game elsewhere. Violence had intruded on the bright morning scene and I felt vaguely responsible, as if we'd brought it with us.

Suddenly, the screams stopped. A familiar American voice pierced the silence. "I think he's had enough." Buck was orchestrating the scene inside the shack. It was true, I thought miserably, we had brought the violence with us.

"You're goddamn right, he's had enough!" Stewart? Cursing? Sure enough, the missionary appeared in the doorway and gazed out into the street. My husband ducked around the side of the shack, to avoid detection, but he needn't have bothered. Unable to endure the frightened stares of the neighborhood's residents, Stewart had lost his nerve.

"That's right," I heard the American say in a placating tone. "You're better off staying with us. We're almost finished here. Then we can all leave together."

"*Najdroższa!*" hissed Jakub from somewhere behind me. Then he was at my side, hustling me away. We veered off the street onto a narrow gully that snaked between the rows of shanties, a dumping ground ankle-deep in refuse, rotting food, human waste. I'd worn shoes that day instead of sandals on account of the rain, but by the time we reached the tourist district, they were ready for the trash. We stopped at the first open air market we saw and bought ourselves cheap sneakers to wear back to the hotel.

"You think he had something to do with the attack on our

convoy?" said my brother over sundowners on the terrace that evening. We were drinking Pastis, a yellow liqueur that turned milky white when you added water. I wasn't crazy about the taste of licorice to begin with, and was still brooding over the ugly scene we'd overheard.

Jakub took a sip from my glass. "The man being tortured? Why else would have Buck been there?"

"I guess you're right." Like me, Gray had no difficulty believing that Mr. Quang conducted this type of interrogation all the time. None of us had forgotten the fixer's insistence that Mankiewicz turn over the footage of the Cao Dai monks' demonstration for the return of their pope. Whatever services he was providing to the production of *The Quiet American*, Mr. Quang was clearly reporting back to his government about anything suspicious. But how did he and Buck come to be working together, my brother wanted to know, and why did they bring in Stewart?

"I can think of several reasons," my husband replied addressing the second of Gray's questions. "For one thing, he'll be more alert to subversive activity in his own area, now that he knows how the Việt Minh operate. I expect they got a full confession out of that man in the shack. He knows what to watch for, and after what he observed, I'd imagine that Stewart will make his parishioners aware of the consequences of collaborating with the Communists. The people around us learned the lesson too," he added grimly. "The consequences for sheltering insurgents are pretty dire. Rather than keeping silent about a neighbor's dealings with the Việt Minh, in the future I expect that somebody will let the authorities know what's going on. That's how it worked in France during the occupation."

That's how it worked behind the Iron Curtain too, I thought, remembering our time in Hungary. There it seemed that half the country was being bribed or coerced into informing on the other half. But I wouldn't categorize Phú Nhuận District as a hotbed of subversive activity. Where would people find the time for political protest, living hand-to-mouth as they did? Surely Buck's lesson was wasted on the poor inhabitants of that neighborhood, I argued.

"Ah, that's where you're wrong," said Gray. He'd learned a fair amount about the neighborhood from Tam. Phú Nhuận was always poor, but its inhabitants weren't always destitute, he told us. They had jobs as factory workers, or they worked on the railroads, the trams, or as stevedores on the docks. A lot of them joined Communist labor unions in the 1930s—they were legal here at the time, just like in mainland France—but unions were outlawed during the war and their members were driven underground.

"Now, here's the incredible thing. Those very union members rose up to take their country back from the Japanese occupiers. They formed workers' militias and battled in the streets—"

"Workers' militias?" Jakub interrupted. "Like the Syndicalists in Spain?"

My brother gave a bitter laugh. "Exactly like the Syndicalists in Spain. And they met the same fate as their counterparts in Madrid, which isn't surprising when you think about it. Hồ Chí Minh spent a great deal of time in Moscow."

"Moscow?" This too was news to my husband. "I thought he started the Việt Minh in China."

"Hồ got around. He was the darling of the Politburo in the 1920s, before Stalin assumed control of the Soviet Communist Party, and he watched how Stalin did it."

"Did what?" I lit a cigarette, steeling myself for another lecture.

Jakub was good enough to enlighten me. "Slaughtered everyone who stood in his way, *najdroższa*." He turned his attention back to Gray. "You learned all this from Tam?" he said skeptically. "He couldn't have been more a child when those events were taking place."

"That's true, but he had a strong incentive to learn what happened, once he was old enough to understand. His father belonged to a Trotskyist militia in Phú Nhuận. After the Japanese surrender, they wanted to form a peoples' government. They'd managed to relieve some of the departing Japanese of their rifles—"

"Trotskyists!" my husband marveled. "In this day and age?"

"You still find pockets of them, here and there. Cara and I were friendly with some Trotskyists in England."

"Well, they were more your friends than mine." I blew a puff of smoke and watched it dissipate in the air above Gray's head. Poor Tam. His radical father had obviously not survived the war. We were similar in that way, losing a parent at such a young age, and it didn't surprise me one bit that he'd gone to the trouble of piecing together the story of how his father died because I'd done exactly the same thing in regard to Vivien. I'd also managed to find a surrogate mother for myself in Italy. What if Tam were simply looking for a father figure and had found one in my brother? Would that be such a terrible thing?

# CHAPTER TWELVE

## The Croix de Sud
## March 2, 1957

"*Najdroższa?*" Jakub turned away from the mirror, looking terribly handsome in his crisply pressed shirt, his thick, dark hair still damp from the shower. "Shall we go?"

I resisted the impulse to unbutton the shirt and lure him to bed. We'd returned, hot and tired, from an afternoon cruise on the Saigon River by sampan to find a note from Laurence inviting us to meet her at a French nightclub that same evening. There was something she wished to discuss, she said, a matter that could not wait. Naturally, my husband was intrigued.

"Coming, darling." I took a last glance around the room, my eyes alighting on Lily's teacups. I'd set them out on top of the bureau and they were so lovely, my own glass forest, I couldn't stop admiring them. Maybe the concubines had been comforted by having such beautiful things commissioned for their exclusive use. It did seem as if they'd been groomed since infancy for life in a gilded prison. If you'd never tasted freedom, would you miss it?

The Croix de Sud had a curved facade, like Magasins

Charner, and sidewalk tables like the Continental. We'd often passed by the building on rue Catinat on our way to the Majestic, but this was the first time we'd ventured inside. Instantly, I was transported to Paris, not to the swank Saint-Germain-des-Prés nightclub scene where the trio and I performed amid white-jacketed waiters who glided between the tables, proffering champagne to well-heeled customers who were there mostly to show off. This was more like the dive in Montparnasse where the fellows and I ended up after we'd finished playing those fancy gigs, a seedy bar whose clientele came for the music—although the music at the Croix de Sud was nothing to write home about. Beneath its dim fluorescent lighting, an all-girl orchestra decked out in satin and feathers and showing a good deal of leg worked their way diligently through a repertoire of French cabaret music, tunes made popular decades ago by Marie Dubas and Édith Piaf. I half expected to see Jean Gabin emerge from the shadows, wearing his trademark silk scarf and fedora. The gangster he played in *Pépé le Moko* would have fit right in.

"Jakub! Cara! *Par ici!*" Peering through the fug of cigarette smoke, we managed to locate Laurence, happily ensconced at a table of French paratroopers. She introduced my husband as "a wartime comrade" and I was gratified by their reactions. Two of them immediately surrendered their seats, while a third asked what we liked to drink and headed straight to the bar.

"*Deux cognacs,*" said Jakub. "*Merci.*"

The airman returned with two snifters of Martell, a high-end brand. I wouldn't have known it was the good stuff, but my husband had a discerning taste for eaux de vie, owing to the family distillery business. Appreciatively, he met the paratrooper's eye over the rim of his glass.

"Cordon Bleu? *Pas mal*," he said, taking another sip.

"*Ils n'ont pas le XO, ou je vous l'aurais proposé.*" The airman was actually apologizing for not having been able to procure the XO, the top-of-the-line cognac! What's more, he expected nothing in return for his tribute beyond a tacit acknowledgment of their common sacrifice for France. With a curt nod, he wished us good night and headed back to the bar with his companions. My last glimpse of them was of three red berets, vanishing into the haze.

Laurence didn't waste any time on small talk. She'd somehow caught wind of the attack on our convoy and demanded a full account: how did we get separated from our escort, was it true that the American had killed a Việt Minh agent, and how was our brother's little friend?

Five days since the ambush, I was still waking up shivering in the middle of the night, the image of the dead soldiers in their jeep vivid and disturbing. The last thing I wanted to do was to relive the experience. But I was impressed by how much she knew. Compared to the assassination attempt on the president, a guerrilla attack in a remote region of the country hadn't merited so much as a paragraph in the daily papers.

"Where did you hear about it?" I blurted out. She must have had inside sources.

"Good question, *najdroższa.*"

The Frenchwoman appeared not to have heard me. Pulling a small notebook from her pocket, and removing the cap from her pen, she got down to business. "*Qu'est-ce qu'ils font, là-bas?*" What are they doing down there?

"*Qu'est-ce qui fait?*" said Jakub. What is who doing?

"*Les Américains, bien sûr.*" The Americans, of course.

My husband leaned back in his chair and folded his arms. "*Demands-tu en tant qu'amie ou en tant que journaliste?*"

152

Are you asking as a friend, or as a journalist? he wanted to know.

Laurence gave him a rueful smile. "*Je suis d'abord journaliste.*" I am a journalist first and foremost.

Compared to the American's deception, her honesty was a breath of fresh air. She was so savvy, I found myself wanting to talk about the incident in the Delta, and about the interrogation we'd overheard. Maybe she'd catch something that we'd missed.

"Do you mind if I speak in English?" I asked.

"*Comment?*" Laurence leaned closer and cupped a hand around her ear in an effort to hear me over the music. The orchestra had launched into rousing rendition of "Non, je ne regrette rien," a new song of Piaf's. We'd heard her perform it at the Olympia in Paris just a few months earlier. I was surprised the song had already made it to Saigon.

Jakub repeated my question in French. "*Ça vous dérange si elle parle en anglais?*"

The journalist shook her head, uncomprehending. "*Venez avec moi,*" she shouted over the din. Picking up her drink, she motioned for us to do the same and began pushing her way to the back of the room. We followed her khaki-clad figure as best we could amid the commotion; every paratrooper in the joint had gotten drunkenly to his feet and was singing along with the chorus. Personally, I preferred "La vie en rose," Piaf's signature tune, but "Non, je ne regrette rien" was the hands-down favorite of this crowd.

We caught up with Laurence outside the manager's office. "Monsieur Hervé?" She rapped sharply at the door. "Monsieur Hervé, *vous êtes là?*"

The door was opened by a small, round gentleman, nearly as wide as he was tall. He resembled a beachball, and a sinister one at that, with his dark eyebrows and downward-turning mustache, but his dour demeanor vanished the moment he saw Laurence. Elated, he indicated that she should stoop down to his level so that he might kiss her on either cheek.

"*Je voudrais présenter mes amis de Paris*," she said when she'd straightened up again, introducing us as her friends from Paris.

The manager now smiled at the two of us. "*Bienvenue à ma petite boîte.*" Welcome to my little nightclub. He was from Paris, he told us, and had worked as a bartender at the Hotel Claridge in the 1930s before coming out to Saigon. Did we know the place?

"*L'hôtel Claridge!*" my husband exclaimed. "*Bien sûr que je le sais. Vous y avez travaillé dans les années trentes, vous dites?*"

"*Mais, oui.*"

"*Avez-vous par hasard entendu la Quintette du Hot Club de France?*"

"*Je les ai vus plusieurs fois.*"

"*Ç'est formidable!*" Jakub was ecstatic. The jazz quintet started by gypsy guitarist Django Reinhardt and the classically trained violinist Stéphane Grappelli, the Hot Club de France, was the inspiration behind his own trio. Not only had Monsieur Hervé seen the musicians perform many times at the Claridge, he'd brought some of their recordings with him to Saigon and offered to play them for us on the spot.

"*Nous ne voulons pas vous déranger,*" said Laurence. We don't want to put you to any trouble: the first words she'd managed to get in edgewise. The manager insisted it would be no trouble at all. He pointed to a mahogany credenza that stood against the far wall and urged us to go over and open it. Inside was a Victrola and an enviable assortment of records.

My husband had no trouble deciding what to play first. "Look at this," he marveled, holding up an ancient 78. The American jazz violinist Eddie South joined Grappelli on the Swing label recording of Bach's double violin concerto, with Django accompanying them on the guitar. From the reverent way he handled the record, I could tell how thrilled he was to hear the three jazz legends improvising on Bach.

Monsieur Hervé commended him on his taste. He placed the record on the turntable, lifted the tone arm off its rest, put down the needle, and cranked up the phonograph, studiously ignoring the French journalist's signs of impatience. Tucked away in his office with the girl orchestra out front butchering the standards, he wasn't about to relinquish this chance to share his collection with a true aficionado.

"*Encore?*" he asked, when the side ended.

Jakub was game, but I could see that Laurence was ready to throttle the nightclub manager. "Maybe we should talk first," I suggested, earning a grateful smile.

The journalist requested a few minutes of privacy in his office, after which we were free to stay all night and listen to Monsieur Hervé's entire collection. Once we were alone, she wasted no time extracting the information she wanted about the ambush: where we were in relation to the resettlement area, how far behind the lead vehicle, how long before we were reunited with the supply trucks. From her questions, we realized that the attack on our convoy fit within a larger pattern. Buck had acknowledged a few "incidents," as he put it, "a bit of unrest," but we now learned that attacks in the Mekong Delta had been taking place on an almost daily basis since the beginning of the year.

"One of my colleagues, he traces these on a map. He finds

they are in the same *secteurs*—I think she is the same word in English?—where is found the Communists. I am sorry. I am not saying so well. You permit me to speak French?"

The majority of the attacks, she proceeded to explain, took place in sectors where Communists had been active during the Indochinese war. Diem was attempting to restore control over the area by sending his own men to replace the local village chiefs, but lacking awareness of the villagers' needs, these government appointees were being removed from their posts.

"*Le gouvernement les rappelle à Saigon?*" my husband asked. The government is recalling them to Saigon?

"*Les gens eux-mêmes les enlèvent.*" The people themselves are removing them. Laurence paused to let the meaning of her words sink in. There was something off-putting in her manner, I thought, although I couldn't put my finger on it. Was she pleased that the situation in the South was deteriorating since the French had pulled out?

Jakub thought so. We were undressing for bed and I'd voiced my suspicion that the journalist didn't want to see the Americans succeed where the French had failed.

"They're too proud even to admit they failed, *najdroższa*. That song we heard in the nightclub, the one the paratroopers were singing . . ." He pulled his undershirt off over his head.

"Je ne regrette rien?"

"Mm-hmm." Wearing only his boxer shorts, he slipped into bed. It was too hot for pajamas.

"What about it?"

"They ought to make it the French national anthem," he said, flicking off the lamp on his nightstand. "The French regret nothing, which is why they're incapable of learning from their mistakes."

I was struck by the bitterness in his voice. He had regrets, I knew. Regrets over having survived while his family perished, but until that moment it had never occurred to me that he might regret his service to France. My husband had risked his life for his adopted country. Had he been picked up by the authorities on one of his courier missions, he surely would have been deported to Auschwitz. Other Jews went into hiding for the duration of the war, or they made for the Swiss or the Spanish border, but he'd seen France as worth fighting for at the time.

"Darling, what's wrong?"

Jakub rolled over onto his back and drew my head onto his chest. He lay so still, I could hear his heart beating. An eternity passed before he spoke. "Forgive me, *najdroższa*. When I remember what it was like, being a foreigner in Paris with the word 'Jew' stamped on my passport, I get angry."

Such a terrible burden, this fury he carried inside. Once or twice I'd glimpsed it without realizing what I was seeing. Now I reviewed the conversation in the Croix du Sud, after Laurence had completed her little interview, seeking insight into my husband's distress. Monsieur Hervé had returned and was insisting on playing another Eddie South and Stephane Grappelli duet for my husband, a 1937 performance of "Dinah" also recorded at the Hot Club de France.

"*Si vous y prêtez attention, vous remarquerez que le nègre a introduit un soupçon de blues dans le deuxième solo.*" If you listen carefully, you'll notice how the Negro has introduced a hint of the blues into the second solo.

Laurence had perked up at the mention of Eddie South's race. "*Un nègre?*" Addressing me directly for the first time, and switching to English, she'd demanded to know why

Americans didn't appreciate our Negro musicians. "In France, we adore them," she'd said.

I'd hardly known where to begin. That same morning, I'd picked up an old issue of *Look* in the Continental's lobby, my eye caught by the cover line beneath the magazine's title: *The Shocking Story of Approved Killing in Mississippi*. But the confession of the two men who murdered Emmett Till could hardly be considered shocking, so common had lynchings become. *Look's* eagerness to pay the killers three thousand dollars for their story was almost as troubling as the lynching itself. Why should they make money from their despicable crime? Till's mother had lost her son and nobody had paid her a nickel.

"I like niggers—in their place—I know how to work 'em. But I just decided it was time a few people got put on notice," one of the killers told the reporter. "Me and my folks fought for this country, and we got some rights."

I'd repeated the man's remarks to Laurence. If I could get her to understand why this white Southerner believed it was his right to make an example of any *nigger* who didn't know his place, she might find it in her to spare some concern for the plight of ordinary people instead of singling out Negro jazz musicians for attention.

"Yes, yes," she'd said dismissively. "It is horrible, the racism in your country."

"You speak as if bigotry did not exist in France," my husband had observed.

"Of course it exists. The stupid people, they are everywhere. You see how many supporters has Poujade in the provinces."

Monsieur Hervé had recognized the name of the populist politician. "*Poujade, quel scélérat!*" he'd exclaimed. Poujade, what a scoundrel!

Laurence had nodded vigorously in agreement. "*Il ressemble à un Nazi, n'est-ce pas?*" He sounds just like a Nazi, doesn't he?

"Not so long ago, a good many French politicians sounded like Nazis," Jakub had pointed out, his voice deceptively mild.

"Oh, you speak of Vichy!" the Frenchwoman had made a moue of displeasure. "But we defeated them, you and I together."

"Did we? I'd have expected a good housecleaning if that were the case, but the last time I looked, the majority of Vichy officials were still at their posts. Some of them have even been promoted."

She couldn't hear what he was saying. The collaborationist regime was an aberration in French history, as far as she was concerned, whereas from Jakub's perspective, little had changed for Jews and foreigners like himself.

"You have a right to be angry," I told my husband, brushing my lips against the stubble on his chin.

"It doesn't scare you, *najdroższa*? It scares me sometimes."

"That's why I'm here," I said. "To chase it away."

# CHAPTER THIRTEEN

## The Disaster Sequence
## March 3, 1957

Jakub was up at dawn, helping the crew set up the equipment in the square in front of the Continental for the disaster sequence. Filming wouldn't begin until mid-morning, but everything had to be perfectly orchestrated because the opening scene, which they'd be shooting overhead from a crane, involved burning cars and exploding gas tanks, with people rushing about in a panic. The production team would be blocking off the square and employing tons of extras, including Tam and me. Gray had arranged for his lover to be among the crowd of Vietnamese onlookers that Fowler shoves his way through in his desperation to get to the milk bar, where he expected to find Phuong among the wounded. Since Redgrave would be in the shot, it was likely they'd get a close-up of Tam as well, and he'd gotten a haircut and bought himself a new shirt, aiming to look his best.

There was no point in primping for the bit part my brother had wangled for me. I'd be lying unconscious in the street by the opera house, enduring the script girl's tearful efforts to revive me. All to no avail: a doctor rushes over, takes one look, and moves on to the next victim. Clearly I am dead. Two orderlies in white smocks lift me onto a stretcher; you get a glimpse of my blood-spattered dress, one arm dangling limply off the edge, as they carry me off screen, accompanied by the sound of the script girl's keening. A memorable scene, even if it required nothing more from me than a willingness to lie motionless, drenched in chocolate syrup (it looks like blood in black and white), while the real drama took place around me. I enjoyed being part of the action.

After changing out of my dress and washing the chocolate syrup off my body, I joined Gray to watch the rest of the filming from his corner room. Mankiewicz wasn't shooting the scenes in order and we had no idea when they'd get to the one with Tam. I was hoping they'd take their time. My brother and I had barely seen one another since we returned from our ill-fated trip to the Delta. He'd been spending his every waking hour with his lover. The Majestic Cinema was showing *To Hell and Back*, the movie version of Audie Murphy's autobiography, in which Murphy plays himself. If I'd had any doubts over Gray's devotion, his willingness to sit through the picture numerous times would have laid them to rest.

He'd been apartment-hunting in Saigon. "I found the perfect place," he told me. "It's on the top floor of that art deco-style building down toward Notre-Dame cathedral on rue Catinat." A French rubber plantation owner was leaving the country and was eager to sell his flat, along with the art collection he'd amassed during his time in Vietnam. As it happened, he knew Lily, having acquired a few pieces from her over the years. Gray thought he might be able to do her a good turn by persuading the man to give over his collection for her to sell on commission, rather than buying it himself. He wanted as little as possible to do with the planter's ill-gotten gains.

"But you'll still be buying his apartment." I couldn't resist needling him a little.

"True." My brother gazed out over the square, absentmindedly stroking his goatee. The crane was being lowered, allowing the cameraman perched on top to return to stable ground. "If you could have seen his face when I took him to see it!" he said.

Doubtless there were other apartments to be had in Saigon that wouldn't have posed such a moral dilemma, but Tam wanted this one, and my brother was too besotted to deny him anything he wanted. Was this the same Gray who'd spoken out as a college student against fascism in Spain? The Gray who refused to name names, who chose exile and a blighted career over betraying his friends? All my life I'd heard him preach about the rights of workers to a living wage and decent working conditions, but according to Ta Philippe, the Khmer who labored on French rubber plantations were treated no better than slaves. Even Buck had condemned the colonialists. Observing my brother's willingness to violate his own principles to keep his lover happy, I felt compelled to say something, to warn him that Tam was not the innocent he appeared to be. The boyishness was just an act—a carefully cultivated act designed to attract lonely men just like him—although I tried to put it less bluntly.

But Gray surprised me. "I know what he is, Cara."

"You do?"

"In Paris, he had nothing to sell but his body. That army officer, his mother's protector? He got Tam into prep school, sure, but then washed his hands of him. He must have known it wouldn't work out. Those places are for the

162

rich and well-connected, just like Yale. If I hadn't had those four years at Choate, I'd have flunked out too. Honestly, it's not what you know, it's who you know and how you carry yourself. They give oral examinations where you're grilled for two hours at a time by a set of professors. The results are preordained: if they like you, they'll lob easy questions, if they don't, they try to trip you up. Tam didn't know a soul in Paris, and on top of this, he was Vietnamese, and not from one of the mandarin families. The other students made his life unbearable. No wonder he cut class to go to the movies."

He didn't need to continue. A beautiful boy sitting alone, day after day, in a darkened movie theater. How long before Tam found his own protector? I envisioned an American, a decent fellow with a sense of fun (I was thinking of the game with the snippets of Western dialogue), probably a Methodist (the hymns). He might have been fresh out of college, doing the grand tour of Europe's cultural capitals before settling down and joining the family business, an aspiring artist following in the footsteps of John Singer Sargent or Edward Hopper. Perhaps he came to Paris to indulge in forbidden pleasures but was repelled by the tawdriness of the Moulin Rouge showgirls, on the one hand, and the forwardness of Pigalle's male prostitutes on the other. Tam's exotic good looks would have been irresistible to any number of men, and I suspected that he hadn't always been treated kindly. After the French defeat at Điện Biên Phủ, life grew difficult for Vietnamese living in France and Lily sent him the airfare to come home. But while I felt sorry for the lost adolescent in Paris, I didn't trust him now. He was too devious by far.

"I have a new job!" Tam announced as he entered the room. While waiting for filming on the scene with Redgrave to begin, he told us, he'd overheard some grumbling among the British crew members. Two of them had gone to Cholon the previous night, looking for an erotic adventure. Unfortunately, the pair solicited the mother and sister of an off-duty policeman, who happened to be standing within earshot. There was a fight, in which the policeman came out the worse for wear. Reinforcements arrived and the Englishmen were arrested. Mr. Quang was dispatched to deal with the situation. Bribes were paid and the Brits were set free, but Mankiewicz threatened to ground the entire crew for the remainder of their time in Saigon to ensure they stayed out of trouble. Tam had approached the fixer to offer his services as an escort and was hired on the spot.

"Pimping for the crew?" I said in disbelief. When was Gray going to face the facts? His young lover was not about to settle down with him in the rubber plantation owner's art deco apartment. Tam was an entrepreneur.

"Cara!" My brother didn't like it when I used rude language.

"You object to the word, but not the act? Pretty hypocritical, if you ask me."

"I didn't ask you, though." Gray's voice was so cold. Tears came to my eyes unbidden, but I dashed them away.

Abruptly I stood up. "Right," I said, fighting back another wave. Tam stepped aside to let me pass as I stumbled my way to the door. He'd remained silent throughout the exchange, but there was no missing the smug look on his face. He was going to break my brother's heart and there was nothing I could do about it.

I was still brooding as I sat in the Continental's shady courtyard later that afternoon, sipping a lemonade. I'd brought along a novel for distraction, one I'd picked up in Orly to read on the flight, *Bonjour Tristesse* by Françoise Sagan. Love, in the view of the world-weary Anne, for all its tenderness, was always accompanied by a sense of loss. Sagan was only seventeen when she wrote the book. So young to have attained such a cynical insight, but by seventeen I'd been no less cynical, having given up my newborn son for adoption after his father, a famous movie actor, refused to have anything more to do with me. I didn't blame Tam for hardening himself against feeling, but I couldn't allow him to manipulate my brother.

"*Elle est là-bas.*" A waiter was pointing me out to Laurence. I'd reached the penultimate chapter of *Bonjour Tristesse* and was a touch annoyed by the interruption, but I invited the journalist to join me and ordered her a lemonade.

"*Ah, j'adore ce livre!*" she exclaimed as she sat down. I love that book! Sagan's second novel, *Un certain sourire*, was nowhere near as good, she warned me. We talked about books until the waiter brought her lemonade. They served it the same way as in Paris: freshly squeezed lemon juice in a tall glass, a bowl of sugar, and a pitcher of water so you could mix it to your own taste.

Laurence took her time mixing hers. She took a sip, added more sugar, and stirred it in. She'd probably been hoping to find Jakub, I realized, but was too polite to ask outright where he was. In fact, I was expecting him, but it would be gauche of me to say so. I spooned more ice into my own glass and waited for her to make up her mind whether to tell me whatever she'd come to tell him.

"I go to the cabin where is the torture," she said. "I go there with a Vietnamese colleague."

"The shack? How did you find it?"

"The shack, yes." It seemed that her hesitation had mostly to do with the gaps in our understanding of one another's languages. The journalist was willing to struggle along in English to make sure I didn't miss anything important.

"We go to the canal in the Phú Nhuận arrondissement. My colleague, he is listening to the people. Some of them, they are talking about it. They are not the ones who are there when it is happening, you understand, but they bring us where is the shack. They know, all the people, but they are afraid, it is so terrible what happens inside. My colleague asks them questions and they will not say to him what they hear."

"*Mais vous les avez persuadés.*" Jakub flashed me a smile as he took a seat at the table. But you persuaded them.

Laurence was visibly relieved to resume her narrative in French. "*Ces gens sont très pauvres.*" Those people are very poor. She and her colleague must have paid for the information.

"*Alors, qu'avez-vous appris?*" So, what did you learn?

The man in the shack was known to be Việt Minh, known as such to his neighbors since the war and now, apparently, to the police. They'd come and carried him off not long after the others left and he hadn't been seen since. As for the interrogation itself, the questions focused on the attack on our convoy. The man had recruited the lead driver, the one whose dead body we'd left by the side of the road— this much he'd conceded freely—but he was reluctant to say who'd tipped him off about the aid shipment. Who was it? Who? Tell us! This was when the beating commenced, to elicit that person's name.

Laurence paused to take a drink of lemonade. She plucked at the petals of a frangipani blossom that had fallen onto our table from a bough overhead, reluctant to resume the narration. I glanced around, thinking that she might be worried about being overheard, but the courtyard was virtually empty. It was coming up on 5 p.m. and people would be gathering at the sidewalk tables out front for an apéritif. Ordinarily we'd be there ourselves, waiting for Gray and Tam to come down and join us, but of course that wouldn't be happening.

"*Continue, s'il te plaît,*" prompted Jakub.

The Frenchwoman looked at me with sympathy. "I am sorry, Cara," she said in English. "I think it is possibly your brother's little friend who goes to the man in the cabin—the shack—and I am telling myself you should know. It is a terrible thing, if he does this. You are maybe all killed. I ask you, is he Việt Minh?"

"Do you mean Tam, my brother's boyfriend? You think he's Việt Minh?"

"*Oui,* Tam. *Je m'excuse,*" she apologized, switching back to French. The man had insisted he didn't know *the boy*; her colleague had noted the word. There was no mistaking the words for "boy" and "man" in Vietnamese, she explained.

Jakub remained skeptical, quizzing the journalist for additional evidence. "*C'est tout? Un mot?*" That's it? One word?

"*C'était simplement une intuition,*" she admitted. It was only a hunch, but hunches couldn't be ignored in her business. "*Nous avons appris cela pendant la guerre, toi et moi.*" You and I learned this during the war.

I wondered whether she wasn't onto something. After she left for the offices of *Le Journal d'Extrême Orient* to file her story, I told my husband what I'd learned that morning about Tam's time in Paris. There was a tightness in my throat when I got to the news of his escort job, but I omitted nothing.

"Gray isn't speaking to me," I concluded in a trembling voice. "It's my fault. I should have held my tongue."

Jakub covered my hand with his own and allowed me to collect myself. "It's only natural for you to care about your brother. To be honest, I don't understand how someone so shrewd about world events could fall prey to an amateur like Tam."

"He's no amateur. Can't you see, he's taunting us!" I couldn't forget that self-satisfied smile. Tam had my brother in thrall and he wanted me to know that it meant nothing to him whatsoever, wielding absolute power over a man's heart. At any moment, and for the most frivolous of reasons, he could end things. And he would, the minute something better came along.

"Taunting us?" my husband said. "How?"

"Do you think it was an accident that you caught him seducing Buck in the Rainbow? He meant for you to see what he was doing and I bet he'd have liked nothing better than for you to tell Gray, just to watch the fireworks. This morning he made it clear that he intends to make my brother miserable. He was daring me to stop him, knowing full well I couldn't."

Jakub was not convinced. "I don't trust him either, but Tam won't risk losing his meal ticket. He might have been hedging his bets, back there in the Rainbow with Buck, but he's got what he wants now, doesn't he? His very own protector. You and I may not approve of such a mercenary arrangement, but if Gray's content to pay for love—"

"He's not in it only for the money." I thought Tam was jaded. He'd been playing the game so long, mere conquest wasn't enough. He wanted spice, and it occurred to me that his taste for intrigue might not be limited to the sexual realm. "What if he'd somehow found out that the aid shipment destined for Cái Sắn contained guns? Imagine the thrill of having that kind of insider's knowledge. The temptation to flaunt it would have been irresistible."

"He's cocky, I'll give you that, but subterfuge takes more

than bravado, *najdroższa*. Overconfidence is a liability in the underground. Believe me, I saw it too many times. His sort don't survive."

"Who said he's going to survive?" I countered. "We were all meant to be killed when the guerrillas opened fire on the convoy. It was sheer luck we got separated from the escort."

"You're saying that Tam could have been the informant without being made privy to the plan." My husband gave a slow, solemn nod. "It makes sense. Otherwise, he'd have been hanging back with the supply trucks, not following us into an ambush."

"Exactly!" I felt vindicated.

"It would explain the fight, too. Tam could have realized he'd been set up and cornered the driver when the American's back was turned, although in that case I'd have expected him to play it safe for a while."

"What do you mean?" Something wasn't sitting right. I could hear it in his voice.

"You say Tam sought out Mr. Quang today on the set?"

"About the escort job, yes."

"Your brother must have told Tam that Buck and Mr. Quang were hunting for the informer. If he had a hand in the ambush, even if he didn't plan it, even if he only set things in motion, he ought to be laying low, not drawing attention to himself. No, *najdroższa*," he said gently, "the tip must have come from the Vietnamese side, some Customs official or government flunky in the pay of the opposition."

My husband thought I was letting my antagonism toward my brother's lover cloud my judgment, but he assumed that everyone was as consistent and straightforward as he was, whereas I saw people as riddled with contradictions. For all his callousness, Buck had a soft side which he'd shown me on the day we went shopping at Magasin Charner. It was hard to square the man who could use a dead body for target practice, the one who'd ruthlessly directed the torture scene we'd overheard, with the shy fellow who had wanted to name his CIA front operation after his mother, and yet he'd managed to arouse my protective instincts.

Tam, on the other hand, was as cold-hearted as they came. I believed he was more than capable of having betrayed us, but could I prove it? The armchair detectives on *The Adventures of Ellery Queen* would narrow down the suspects on the weekly radio program in accordance with three criteria: means, motive, and opportunity. They almost always fingered the wrong culprit, but Father and I would allow ourselves to be swayed by their reasoning. Then, after the ad for Bromo-Seltzer, when Ellery Queen revealed the correct solution to the mystery, we'd go back over the evidence to figure out where we'd been led astray.

Over the course of the following days, having little else to occupy my mind while lounging around the Majestic's pool, waiting for Jakub to get off work, I reviewed the evidence of Tam's duplicity. Did he have the means to betray us? I still thought that Buck might have let it slip that the aid shipment contained guns, or it was possible that Tam had ferreted out the information himself while perusing the Customs documents. The American had come to rely on him to negotiate with the Vietnamese officials. As for opportunity, the man in the shack claimed he didn't recognize the informant, but even if he were telling the truth, Tam could have known that the man in the shack was Việt Minh. His father had been a Communist labor organizer in Phú Nhuận before the war, I recalled. Maybe the man in the shack had been one of Tam's father's associates. He could have been a Trotskyist who'd subsequently changed allegiances, whether out of conviction or expedience, when he realized that Hồ Chí Minh's movement was the only viable opposition to the French.

Motive remained the sticking point. Laurence had asked whether Tam was Việt Minh, but here I had to concede that this was unlikely. He was too young to have fought with the insurgency and besides, he'd been in Paris for much of the time. Lily had sent him away and hadn't summoned him home until the war ended.

Lily. Where else would Tam have acquired his skill at manipulation, if not at his mother's knee? Her courteousness toward us in their apartment had eclipsed the memory of her brusque behavior the previous day. The real Lily, I'd convinced myself, was the gracious hostess who'd served us coffee and made us a gift of the glass forest that now adorned my dresser. Naturally she'd been distraught when we barged in with the news that her son had been seriously injured. What mother wouldn't have been upset, under the circumstances? Jakub and I not only forgave her, we'd taken her part when we saw how Tam bullied her. But now I wondered if we hadn't been duped.

Lily traded in charm. That and beauty were the only commodities she possessed, and her success in attracting and holding a protector like the French officer for as long as she did was proof of her skill. Did that skill extend to political intrigue? Why had she been so eager to send Tam to Paris at the tender age of sixteen? Was she looking to get him away so she'd be free to work on behalf of the Việt Minh without having to fear for his safety? Perhaps there was more to the liaison with Guillaume than met the eye. She could have been using sex to extract military secrets, upcoming army maneuvers, bombing targets, and the like. It was hard to imagine Tam's mother as a Vietnamese Mata Hari, but I couldn't dismiss the theory without talking to her again. I'd had enough sun for the day, Jakub was tied up until evening, and my brother was avoiding me. Why not pay a little visit to the antique shop?

Lily welcomed me like an old friend. She was just thinking of me, she said. Would I allow her to buy me a coffee? Business was slow, and there was something urgent she wished to discuss in private. She had a friend who could translate for us, if I had trouble following her French.

"*Ce nest pas loin*," she said. "*Il y a un raccourcie.*" It isn't far. There's a shortcut. We walked from her shop to Ben Thanh Market, entering by the main gate and emerging from a side entrance a block from Gia Long Street, a grand boulevard flanked with tamarind trees. Catty-corner from the palace where the French had established their colonial headquarters sat a tiny brasserie, La Marseillaise. A sign on the door said it was closed until dinnertime, but Lily barged right in, greeting the French proprietor with a kiss on either cheek. I thought he might be another one of her conquests, but then he called to his wife Denise, a Vietnamese woman, to come out from the kitchen and I realized that it was she who'd nabbed him.

Lily introduced me to the two of them in French and ordered iced coffees, then she and her friend embarked upon a lengthy conversation in Vietnamese. Denise spoke English well enough to give me a précis. Lily had just learned that Gray intended to stay in Saigon, she told me, and wanted me to persuade him to take her son with him to England before he got himself in trouble.

"What kind of trouble?" I said sharply. Denise relayed my question in Vietnamese, but Lily had picked up on my tone and insisted on answering me in French.

"*Ils essaient de le recruter, le Việt Minh.*" The Việt Minh are trying to recruit him.

"*Qu'est-ce qui te fait penser ça?*" What makes you think that?

Lily ran her finger absently along the rim of her glass. *Ils sont venus le voir,*" she said quietly. "*C'était le soir même qu'il est rentré de l'hôpital.*" They came to see him. The very evening he came home from the hospital.

"*Ils sont arrivés à l'improviste? Comment en ont-ils entendu parler?*" I asked in disbelief. They appeared out of the blue? How did they hear about it?

She shrugged. "*Le monde est tout petit.*" It's a small world.

Not that small, I thought to myself, trying to tamp down my excitement. My theory about Tam wasn't so farfetched after all. He *was* in contact with the Việt Minh. Just to make certain, I asked Denise how Lily knew they were Việt Minh. It wasn't as if they wore badges.

They weren't strangers, came the reply. They were Tam's old school friends. The four of them had been inseparable as boys and she'd recognized them instantly. Denise now took it upon herself to relate the story of how Tam had landed in Paris. He and the other students at his Saigon lycée had gone on strike to protest the French occupation of their country. One of them was killed when the police opened fire on a demonstration they'd staged right over there. She pointed to the Governor's Palace across the street. His mother had begged Tam to keep away—the authorities were hunting down the radicals and throwing them in penal camps—but he'd refused to take her advice.

"*C'est un romantique, comme son pére,*" Lily interjected. He's a romantic, like his father.

Denise confirmed this statement. Tam idolized his father. They'd all had such hopes for him when he passed the entrance exam for Pétrus Ký! Surely I'd noticed how clever he was. With his gift for languages, his teachers were encouraging him to pursue a career in law or business. Instead, he'd become ensnared in revolutionary politics and had Lily not prevailed upon Guillaume to send him to Paris, Tam might very well have met the same fate as his father. Now they feared he was being drawn back into that treacherous world, and the only solution was to get him away.

Throughout this conversation, Denise's husband had remained behind the bar, polishing the glassware and otherwise occupying himself, but now he came over to our table to offer his succinct opinion on the situation. *"Les communistes tuent les leurs."* The Communists kill their own.

Motive, means, and opportunity were all in place, but unlike Ellery Queen, I took no satisfaction in having my suspicions confirmed. Viewing Tam through his mother's eyes, I saw how my brother might have recognized himself in his young lover and my heart went out to Tam. He was bright and passionately dedicated to his cause, a crusader. Who knows what he might have become, had he not been preyed upon in Paris? Like poor Kiêu, he'd had no choice but to succumb to circumstance.

*"Alors,"* said Lily, *"tu comprends?"* You understand now, don't you? Taking my two hands between her own, she entreated me to make sure that my brother took Tam out of Vietnam as soon as possible. *"Et cette fois il ne doit pas revenir."* And this time he must not come back.

# CHAPTER FOURTEEN

## Singin' in the Rain
## March 8, 1957

I waited until breakfast to tell Jakub about the conversation with Lily. We'd wound up on a cruise on the Saigon River the night before with some of the crew. Between the buffet dinner, the dancing girls, and the Vietnamese musicians' energetic renditions of Dizzy Gillespie tunes, both of us were exhausted by the time we got back to the room.

"You promised her, *najdroższa*? After what happened down there? We all could've—well, you know what I'm saying." Givral was crowded, as usual, and we were speaking in vague terms. You never knew who might be within earshot.

I did know what he was saying, but I also knew what would happen to Tam if he stayed. Whether or not he had a role in planning the attack on our convoy now seemed beside the point. Sooner or later he'd join the fight; it was in his nature to stand up against tyranny, one of the finer aspects of his character.

"Is his fight so very different from yours?" I said.

Jakub grimaced. "In substance, maybe not. But ours was more clear-cut."

"That's why we need to convince him to leave." I took a bite of my croissant. Lily's news that Tam had been visited by his Việt Minh friends also gave me an olive branch, a way of making peace with my brother. Five days had gone by since our argument and I ached to set things right between us. Enlisting him in the effort to bring Tam out of Vietnam would put us back on the same side.

After my husband set off for his last day of work, I went straight back to the hotel and climbed the stairs to room 214. Gray opened the door in his bathrobe, fresh out of the shower.

"Cara!" The next thing I knew, he was hugging me as if we'd been estranged for months, not days. "Come in before I make a spectacle of myself," he said, drawing me out of the dim corridor.

I was wearing a sleeveless white top, to show off my tan, and polka-dot capri pants I'd found in Magasins Charner, knock-offs of a pair I'd seen on Brigitte Bardot in *Vogue*. *And God Created Woman* had opened in Paris at the end of November and there were photos of her everywhere.

"Very nice," said Tam languidly from Gray's bed. "You look just like her."

This was so patently untrue that I had to laugh, which did serve to break the ice. I had to admit, they seemed happy, lounging around half-naked in their private world. It would be nowhere as easy for them to maintain this equilibrium in London. A villa in the south of Italy might be a better choice. A number of writers and film people had second homes on the island of Capri or in one or another of the ritzy towns along the Amalfi coast. Italians were more live-and-let-live, at least when it came to wealthy foreigners. I wouldn't mind visiting them on the Amalfi coast, either. The views were supposed to be stunning.

Gray threw on some clothes and accompanied me upstairs while Tam got himself bathed and dressed. Once we were in my room, with the door closed, I told him what I'd learned from Lily about Tam's Việt Minh visitors. I'd been afraid he'd accuse me of meddling, going to Tam's mother behind his back, but he was grateful for the information. It explained a lot, he said.

"What do you mean, *explains a lot*?"

My brother sat on the edge of the unmade bed and patted the space beside him. "I thought he was seeing other men," he said in a low voice. "The signs were too plain to miss: mysterious calls at random times during the day or night. If I answered, they'd hang up."

"They called your room at the Continental?"

He nodded. "The other night we were at the Rainbow, having a drink with some of the lads before Tam took them out carousing. I noticed a Vietnamese fellow hovering by the entrance, watching our table. He wasn't dressed for an evening out and the maître d' probably wouldn't let him in, but Tam saw him and something passed between them. I pretended not to notice, but he was very late coming home. He fell into bed, too tired even for . . ." Gray cleared his throat. "Anyway, the next night—last night, it was—none of the lads from the crew showed up."

I explained about the spur-of-the-moment cruise. "They were all three sheets to the wind by the time we docked."

"Well, it definitely threw a monkey wrench into his plans. He kept checking the time, and when I suggested going back to our room and making an early night of it, he told me to go on ahead. He thought he might have gotten his signals crossed and said he was going to stop off in one of the places the lads liked, to make sure they hadn't gone there directly. He put me in a pedicab, but I hopped out after a block and hot-tailed it back to the Rainbow. I was sure he'd arranged an assignation and I wanted to catch him in the act."

"You followed him in Chinatown?" I said. "What if he'd seen you?"

"By then I was past caring. I'm not proud of myself," he admitted.

I made a sympathetic noise, imagining only too well the state he'd been in. "What happened next?"

"He took a roundabout route, down one alley, doubling back a few blocks over. We passed the same massage parlor several times. Those dives all look alike, but I noticed this one because of its name. The Golden Lotus. A neon sign in the window had it in English, only the 'G' was burned out, so it read 'olden Lotus.' I was beginning to think he was lost, but then he surprised me by going inside.

"I figured it was time to give up and get myself back to one of the bigger avenues, where I could pick up a cab, but I had no idea where I was. While I was trying to get my bearings, an old Chinese man came up and offered to sell me some opium, right on the spot. A Westerner in Cholon at that time of night could only be looking for one of two things. The Golden Lotus sold one of them. He was selling the other."

Was Gray going native? "Don't tell me you took him up on the offer."

"At first I refused, but he wouldn't take no for an answer." A note of pride entered his voice. "I haggled him down to a ridiculously low price. We shook hands on it. Do you know how they do these things on the street? The dealer carries a small, hand-held scale. He showed me how it worked, insisted I put the weights on the one side while he measured out the quantity of opium we'd agreed on—"

"Cut to the chase," I urged. My brother was a screenwriter. He knew how to draw out a story for maximum dramatic effect.

Gray ignored me. "We were both crouched on the sidewalk. The man was ancient and he was taking an eternity to weigh out the drug. It was painful on my knees, squatting like that. We'd only just reached the point of exchanging money when the door opened and Tam came out. He wasn't alone, he was with three fellows his age, and they seemed to be in no particular hurry. You can believe I took my time, counting out the piastres. I wanted to stay low, with my head down, away from the light of that damn neon sign. Lucky thing I was carrying a lot of small bills. It was like paying in pennies."

"Lucky thing," I echoed. The whole scene was like something out of a B-movie, one of the bad ones that played on stereotypes of Asian decadence.

"The dealer was very patient, I'll say that for him. Considerate, too. Tam and his friends finally went their separate ways and I was worried about getting home. He walked me back to the tourist area and hailed me a taxi."

I laughed despite myself. "He must have thought you were desperate to get home for your fix." Gray's story did lend strength to Lily's contention that her son was being drawn into the insurgency against his will. Tam might be glad to quit Vietnam for a spell, I suggested, put some distance between himself and his former schoolmates. Southern Italy was delightful in the spring, before the tourist season began.

"You've got it all figured out, eh?" My brother patted my head. "Seriously, though. He was pretty wound up when he got home. I suggested a pipe, to calm him down."

"Didn't he wonder how you came by the drug?"

"We've smoked before. He's expert at preparing them.

179

We keep a kit with all the paraphernalia in the room. I just added what I bought to the stash."

Something else to worry about, I thought: Gray becoming an opium fiend.

We made plans to meet for sundowners on the terrace and have dinner together afterwards. Mankiewicz was hosting the wrap party that evening and I didn't expect to see Jakub before midnight, which left me with a good many hours to fill. I resigned myself to spending some of them sunbathing at the Majestic, but on the way into the hotel, I noticed they'd changed the program at the cinema. *Singin' in the Rain* was playing and I bought a ticket for the early matinee. What better way to spend the hottest part of the day than watching Gene Kelly dance? He made it look effortless, but I knew how much work it took to achieve that effect. Getting caught in a cloudburst without an umbrella on my way home didn't dampen my spirits one bit. I found myself splashing through puddles while humming the title song, laughing at clouds, turning my face upwards to let the warm rain wash away my cares.

"Miss Walden! What luck, running into you." Buck fell into step beside me as I crossed the square in front of the Continental. I was still being Gene Kelly and hadn't paid attention to who it was heading toward me underneath the big black umbrella. In contrast to the rain, his appearance dampened my spirits instantly.

"Good afternoon, Mr. Polk." I quickened my pace.

The American chuckled as he took in my sodden state. "I'd offer you my umbrella, but I'm afraid it's too late." He himself was dressed in a suit and tie, pants sharply creased as if they had just been ironed. He must have come straight from home to be looking so crisp in this downpour.

"Yes," I said. "I need to get inside and dry off."

"This won't take but a minute." Buck stopped walking, forcing me to halt as well. He pulled an envelope from his inner vest pocket and proffered it with a ceremonious little bow. "I was intending to leave this for you with the desk clerk, but I'm happier to present it in person. Will you believe me when I tell you how very sorry I am for dragging you into that terrible business in the Delta? I had no right to involve an innocent girl like yourself in something so dangerous."

The envelope contained a check for two hundred dollars issued by the Flora Trade Alliance and made out to me. "I can't accept this," I protested. "It's too much." Was he trying to buy me off?

"Nonsense. You did your country a service, Miss Walden. You, your husband, and your brother. Not to mention young Tam. How is he, by the way? Back on his feet, I trust." The good eye had begun to flutter.

"Yes."

"Glad to hear it. Would you mind asking him to stop by the office? I'd like to compensate him for his work and his trouble."

I kept my face impassive. "I'm not sure I'll see him before we go," I lied.

"Well, here's my business card, in case you do run into him." The good eye was now twitching furiously. His tell. "He can call me at either number. The switchboard at Bachelor Officers' Quarters is manned twenty-four hours a day because of the time difference back home."

The card went in my purse, right next to the American's check. If Gray hadn't managed to convince his lover to leave Vietnam with us on Monday, I was pretty sure this token would clinch it. Tam would be well-advised to lay low until then.

Back in the room, I toweled off and hung my wet clothes and bathing suit over the tub. I decided to put the remaining time until cocktail hour to productive use by emptying the closet and bureau drawers of clothing I didn't anticipate Jakub or myself wearing in the upcoming days, laying everything out on the bed to see which items could be packed and which needed laundering. While cleaning out my spare purse—my secretary purse—I found the key to Buck's office. How long before he remembered I had it? I didn't want to give him an excuse to look me up again, but maybe I could return it while he was out. The rain had stopped and a short walk would do me good. I could even drop off a few articles at the dry cleaner's next door. I took the precaution, however, of calling the office before setting off and was reassured when he didn't answer the phone.

The second floor was no longer deserted. Emerging from the stairwell, I heard a buzz of activity: a phone ringing, the clacking of typewriter keys punctuated by a ding and the ratcheting sound as the carriage hit the end of a line. In less than two weeks, the American's operation had expanded into several of the neighboring suites. The Flora Trade Alliance was coming into its own. Scraps of conversation floated past me as I continued down the corridor, American voices—thankfully none I recognized as Buck's, although to be on the safe side I tapped on his door. Receiving no answer, I let myself into my former office.

The room was just as I'd left it, cramped but pleasant enough with the decorative touches I'd added. No doubt the American would find himself a proper secretary like the one down the hall, whose energetic typing was still audible, but my replacement would find things tidy, whereas Buck's desk, which I could see through the connecting door, was uncharacteristically cluttered. Curiosity piqued, I walked over to get a closer look.

Someone had been keeping tabs on Tam at the American's behest. I leafed through a series of typewritten reports going back several days, beginning on the evening after the disaster shoot, when "the subject" was observed taking a contingent of the crew into a series of Cholon brothels—an action he repeated the following night—and continuing right up through the rendezvous at the massage parlor. Tam's circuitous route from the Rainbow to the (G)olden Lotus was noted, along with the time he entered the building (10:17 p.m.) and the number of minutes he spent inside (twenty-three). My brother's presence on the scene was not mentioned, whereas full descriptions were provided of the "three Vietnamese associates" in whose company "the subject" was seen leaving. When the group split up, the report's author made the decision to follow one of Tam's companions. "Subject B" was tracked to a bar on An Bình Street, but managed to give the observer the slip. Tam himself was clocked in at the Continental at 11:08 p.m.

All of this was troubling enough, but accompanying the written account of Tam's doings were a dozen or so black-and-white photographs taken surreptitiously of various locales mentioned in the report, and my brother was discernible in two of them. A sequence featuring Tam and his pals conversing on the sidewalk in front of the (G)olden Lotus included a long-range shot in which I could make out the shadowy forms of Gray and the opium dealer in the bottom left-hand corner of the frame. I spotted my brother's profile in another photo. He was slightly out-of-focus in this one, which caught Tam mid-stride, crossing the street, but Gray's height, coupled with his plaid shirt and khaki pants, pegged him as a Westerner. An astute observer wouldn't have much difficulty connecting him with the other image on this basis, and either photograph could be enlarged, of course, to make identification easier. Once that was done, my brother's goatee would be a dead giveaway.

I needed to think, and I needed to get out of the office immediately. Buck was quite fastidious. It wasn't like him to leave sensitive material strewn about for all to see. He must be intending to come back, I realized, trying not to panic. There was no longer any question of my returning the key. I'd just have to keep my fingers crossed that he wouldn't remember I had it until we were long gone and that he hadn't yet made an inventory of the photos because I wasn't about to leave behind the two in which Gray figured. I stuffed the incriminating evidence into the envelope containing the American's check, which was still in my handbag, and made my way stealthily along the corridor, down the stairs, and out onto the street. Was it paranoia, or did one of the pedicab drivers slouched in the passenger seat of his vehicle perk up as I exited the building? Did he signal to the fellow smoking a cigarette on the opposite side of the street? I hadn't noticed either of them when I'd come out of the dry cleaner's. How long had they been stationed outside the building?

*Stay calm*, I told myself. *Act like nothing's wrong.*

I stepped off the curb, then pretended to have second thoughts about venturing into the traffic and abruptly turned back, proceeding distractedly along the sidewalk. Out of the corner of my eye, I saw the man flick his cigarette away. Languidly he trailed me, matching my pace, remaining on his side of the street as if expecting me to make another foray. I encouraged him in this assumption by pausing every so often to scan for a break in the unending flow of cars, motorcycles, bikes, and scooters, never quite gathering up the nerve, it seemed, to make the leap. In fact, I had a clear destination in mind, and a strategy for losing him. The east gate to Ben Thanh Market was on my side of the street, a little farther down the block. I could dart right in, put some distance between myself and my pursuer, who would then be forced to ford the stream of traffic while I escaped into the crowd of shoppers.

Another feint on my part, but this time I made the mistake of looking back to see whether the man was still on my tail. A part of me was questioning whether I hadn't imagined the whole scenario. Maybe my alleged pursuer was paying attention to me simply because I'd aroused his interest. A young American woman on her own stood out in Saigon under any circumstances, and he might have interpreted my repeated glances in his direction as come hither looks because he suddenly took it upon himself to cross the street. Was he going to apprehend me, or proposition me? Our eyes locked, and in that fleeting contact I saw not the tender gaze of a would-be Lothario, but the rage of a predator whose quarry was on the verge of slipping away.

I ran for it. Ducking inside the entrance, I zigzagged through the clothing aisles, past the knickknacks, the enameled rice bowls, souvenir ashtrays, and ceramic Buddhas. Along the way, I managed to acquire (without any attempt at bargaining) a conical bamboo hat and a cheap shawl. I was short enough to pass for Vietnamese at a distance. Keeping my head down to hide my face, shawl wrapped around my shoulders, I adopted the shuffling gait of a peasant woman, embracing the role for all I was worth. Accustomed to the outdoor market of the neighboring village, she would be overwhelmed by the size of Ben Thanh, not to mention the variety of goods on display, but she would not be hurried into making a purchase. Which stall sold the nicest fabric at a price she could afford? Where might she find notions: buttons, thread, needles, and rickrack? Cannily, she would observe the transactions at the handful she selected for a good while, circling back around as she narrowed down her choices. But shopping was hungry work. Might she not permit herself a small treat, to fortify herself before venturing into the serious business of negotiating for the items she wanted?

The pancake vendor was amused by my disguise, but her smile vanished when she perceived my distress. "*Mademoiselle, s'il vous plaît.*" Stepping outside her stall, she drew me back around with her, patting my arm and repeating the French words for "please" as she encouraged me to sit down on the stool she kept tucked in a corner for her own use. Grateful that I could abandon my role— although I was not ready to abandon my disguise—I replied with the Vietnamese words for "thank you," which I remembered because they sounded like you were saying "come on" in a singsong tone. My rescuer nodded her acknowledgment and returned to serving customers at the counter.

I took advantage of the sanctuary to plot my next move. The idea of Buck just happening to cross paths with me outside the Continental in the pouring rain strained credibility. Somebody must have tipped him off that I'd gone to the cinema, most likely the same person—or persons; evidently they worked in teams—who'd noted the time of Tam's comings and goings for the report. I imagined the American peering out from the shelter of the ornate pillars of the opera house (he'd come from that direction), prepared to stride forth when he caught sight of me returning from the matinee. Watching me skip down the street may have confirmed him in his conviction regarding my innocence, but this would change once he got back to the office and learned of my escapades from the surveillance crew out front. I didn't think there was another woman fitting my description in all of Vietnam.

I had to assume that the Continental was being watched, and that I myself would be a target of surveillance from now on, in addition to Tam. Gray might not be on the radar yet, but if he were seen sipping sundowners on the terrace with the two of us this evening, Buck might begin to suspect a full-blown conspiracy.

It wasn't quite cocktail hour. Still time to get a message to my brother asking him to meet me somewhere else, somewhere private, and to leave Tam behind at the hotel for his own safety. Who could I find and where would that be? The messenger would have to speak English, and the place needed to be close by. I'd look like a lunatic, going about in public wearing the hat and shawl, but I couldn't risk being spotted. The shorter the distance I had to travel, the better. Idly, I wondered if I might succeed in passing myself off as French. I could probably find a beret at one of the stalls and stroll through the streets belting out the Marseillaise. They'd welcome me with open arms at the Croix de Sud.

Funny how the mind works overtime when you're desperate. La Marseillaise was the name of the little brasserie on Gia Long Street where Lily had taken me, and we'd cut through the market to get there. Her friend Denise spoke decent English and would be amenable to fetching my brother from the Continental, once I explained the situation. I'd feel right at home. Denise's husband had decorated the dining room with paintings evoking his native Provence, fields of sunflowers and lavender interspersed with Mediterranean scenes of sun-splashed ports. Above the bar hung a ceramic plaque that bore a charming little saying in Provençal. *Per èstre urous, n'ès que de s'en creire.* To be happy, it is enough to think you are.

If only it were so easy.

# CHAPTER FIFTEEN

## La Marseillaise

"Cara, are you sure this was necessary?" My brother's first words, spoken as he came through the kitchen door of the restaurant.

I looked up from paring carrots. Denise had conveyed my sartorial instructions to the letter, I was glad to see: white shirt, dark pants, no goatee. The shiny chin was rather prominent, given his tan, but a little powder would do the trick.

"What did Tam say?" I asked.

Gray was determined to lighten my mood. "He doesn't like me clean-shaven."

"I meant about the plan, wise guy. Is he prepared to leave with us on Monday?"

"He was already on board before Denise came with your news." They'd gone to Air France after lunch to buy his ticket, stopping off at the antique shop on the way back to tell Lily. "She took it quite stoically. Tam was the one who broke down, although he waited until we were alone. Poor devil. He might never see her again."

"At least he's got you to take care of him, this time," I pointed out.

Denise's husband was at the stove, tending to the bouillabaisse. "*Les carottes?*" he said, recalling me to my

189

duties. Denise had donned an apron and was using a mortar and pestle to mash garlic for the rouille. I was in charge of the crudités and at the rate I was going, the first course wouldn't be ready before the stew.

"Here, let me help." Gray grabbed the mandolin and set to work julienning. As the pile of vegetables dwindled, I related the afternoon's events, starting with the not-so-chance encounter with Buck outside the Continental in the rain and culminating with my escape into the market. I tried to make light of the terror I'd felt when it dawned on me that I was being followed.

"Remember the downtrodden peasant woman Luise Rainer played in *The Good Earth?* I looked just like her."

My brother wasn't buying it. "Whatever possessed you to go to the office? You could have put the stupid key in an envelope and mailed it to him, for God's sake!"

I put down the paring knife and reached for my pocketbook. My fingers were slick with carrot juice, but I managed to pry open the clasp, extracting the photographs by their edges and handing them over without comment.

"Jeez, it's worse than I thought." Involuntarily, Gray's hand went to his chin. "Is this all of them?"

"All the ones with you in them, although Buck might have taken some with him." Also, there would be a set of negatives, I was thinking. If Buck had those, we were sunk. Even now he might be analyzing the evidence with his CIA cronies, making plans to bring us all in for questioning. Consorting against one's own government was a treasonous offense, wasn't it?

Jakub would probably say I was letting my imagination run away with me. If anyone could get us out of this mess it was him, but short of crashing Mankiewicz's party, there was no way of reaching him. I couldn't risk attracting Mr.

Quang's notice; the fixer was awfully shrewd and, for all I knew, he might be keeping an eye on my husband, whether at the American's urging or on his own initiative. The sensible course would have been to stay put, but Gray was anxious about Tam—an anxiety Denise and her husband shared. They didn't trust him to stay in the hotel room. Under the cover of darkness, they feared he would slip out to meet his friends.

"You think he needs babysitting," I said. "Very well. We can go back now."

The sun was setting and the coral sky was smudged with charcoal when we left La Marseillaise. Denise's husband had insisted on feeding us before we left, opening a bottle of Pouilly-Fuissé just for the two of us, the perfect wine to accompany the bouillabaisse. My brother and I were feeling more relaxed as we made our way to the Continental. If there were any watchers in the plaza, I told him, I couldn't spot them. Not that it would have mattered. All we were doing was going into our hotel. Let them report that.

"They wouldn't have recognized me anyhow," he replied with a grin. "I'm innocuous now."

Gray rode the elevator with me up to the third floor and made me wait while he checked my room. "All clear," he said, giving me a peck on the cheek. "Be sure to lock yourself in. After your exciting day, I'd recommend tucking in early. I'm just downstairs, if you need me."

"Thanks." Ordinarily I resisted such brotherly advice, but I was having difficulty keeping my eyes open. I transferred the piles of clothing from the bed to a suitcase, turned off the lights, and lay down. I was roused by a knock at the door. The bedside clock said half past ten. I'd slept for two hours and was still groggy as I went to let Jakub in, happy that he'd managed to get away a little earlier than expected.

Tam stood like a penitent in the corridor. "Cara, I need your help."

"What's the matter?" My heart was pounding. "Did something happen to Gray?"

"Your brother's fine. He's sound asleep."

Gray was sleeping? His sole reason for coming back was to keep an eye on his lover and here he'd gone and let down his guard.

"May I come in?" Tam said.

"Oh, sorry." I stood aside and he brushed past, carrying the scent of sweet tea and hazelnuts into the room. It seemed to emanate from his clothes. Opium. "You drugged him, didn't you?"

Tam was leaning against the wall by the bureau, refusing to meet my eyes. "He won't approve of what I'm about to do."

"And what makes you think I will?"

His words came in a rush. "The police showed up at my mother's shop this evening. They want me to rat on my friends. She thinks it's the only way they'll allow me to fly out of here with you on Monday. If I don't turn myself in, they'll arrest me and extract the information by force. They threatened her, too," he added.

On top of his concern for his mother's safety, I was moved by Tam's fear of losing my brother's respect, although Gray could hardly blame him for naming names, under the circumstances. McCarthyism ruined many lives, but the punishment for fellow travelers back home, while severe, was nowhere near as draconian as it was here in Diem's Vietnam.

"What do you want me to do?" I expected him to ask for Jakub's assistance in spiriting Lily out of the country. My husband was expert at such things, and he could probably count on Laurence's assistance.

Tam reached for the phone on the bedside table. "Call the American and tell him I've agreed to confess. He gave you his home number, didn't he?"

"You can't be serious," I said. "Buck's the one who's been having you followed. You know he's in league with the government."

"I trust him more than the police. If you won't call him, I'll do myself."

I retrieved Buck's business card from my purse and handed it to him without a word. Tam picked up the receiver and asked for an outside line. I listened as he dialed, praying that the American was still attending the diplomatic reception or whatever it was he'd gotten dressed up for. Where in God's name was Jakub?

"Hello, sir. Yes, it's me. Young Tam," he chuckled. "Cara said you wanted to see me. Yes, sir. I'm feeling much better, thank you. I understand. That's very kind, but you know what John Wayne said: 'Never apologize, mister, it's a sign of weakness.' That's right. *She Wore a Yellow Ribbon.* Very good, sir. Tonight? Okay. No, I haven't forgotten about the back entrance. Number twelve."

Clearly this wasn't their first after-hours tryst. "You're planning to seduce him," I said when he hung up.

"I won't have to seduce him. I know when a man wants me." Tam's voice was laced with scorn. Turning, he caught sight of the concubines' teacups. With an angry gesture, he swept them off the bureau.

Bleu de Hué. The porcelain vessels lay shattered on the floor. I stooped to pick up a shard of mountains furred with pines. Behind me, I heard the door close. Still holding the fragment of painted china, I went out on the balcony and watched Tam emerge, his small figure briefly illuminated by the lights of the hotel. He paused at the corner, hesitant. Was he having second thoughts? A minute went by. Then, squaring his shoulders as if bracing himself for an ordeal, he ventured across rue Catinat. As he approached the curb on the opposite side of the boulevard, I saw three forms materialize out of the shadows beneath the overhang at the entrance to Givral. They hung back, waiting for him to pass, then fell into step a few paces behind him. I watched the four until they were out of sight.

Now I had something new to worry about. What would happen when Tam got to the office? Would they follow him inside? The American wouldn't hesitate to shoot if confronted, but Tam's friends might also be armed. It was up to me to stop it, but how? I didn't dare venture into a showdown alone. I needed someone with Jakub's finesse, his war-honed instincts. Someone with a thirst for adventure who could muster reinforcements on short notice. At eleven o'clock at night, I had a pretty good idea where to find her.

Laurence surveyed Buck's office building from opposite the dry cleaner's. "You say to me there is a back door?" We'd already established that the front door was locked, and no lights burned on the second floor.

"Yes." I repeated what I'd heard Tam say about remembering to use the back entrance and she conveyed this information to the two paratroopers who'd accompanied us from the Croix de Sud.

"*On y va!*" said one to the other. Let's go! They sprinted down the block and around the corner. Moments later they returned, giving us the thumbs-up, and beckoned for us to follow. A narrow alley ran behind the buildings, the service entrance to each establishment marked with a painted number. The door to number twelve was slightly ajar. Cautiously we went inside, the paratroopers taking the lead. They'd each brought flashlights, but they shone the beams downward, to keep us from attracting notice as we made our way to the stairwell and ascended to the second floor.

"*C'est où, le bureau?*" Where is the office?

I fished the key out of my pocketbook. "*Au coin. Voici la clé.*" In the corner. Here's the key. Laurence took it and instructed me to wait in the stairwell while she and the paratroopers went to investigate the office. She was truly in her element. From the instant I'd found her in the bar and recounted my dilemma, she could barely manage to repress her excitement. "*La guerre. A nouveau,*" she'd exclaimed as we set off. War again. But the buoyancy had vanished by the time she returned.

"I regret, we are too late," she said dolefully.

"Too late!" I steeled myself for the worst. "What happened?"

"Perhaps it is better you do not see."

Part of me was tempted to take the easy way out she was offering, but whatever had transpired in that office was my fault. "No," I told her. "I must see it for myself."

Laurence shrugged. "*Comme tu le souhaites.*" As you wish.

The paratroopers stood blocking the door, like sentries, but they stepped aside to let us through. Beneath the glare of the overhead light, Buck lay slumped on the rug in front of the conference table, naked from the waist down, his pants bunched around his ankles. The desk lamp we'd purchased for him at Magasin Charner was on the floor, unplugged. Its cord had been used to strangle him.

I froze and covered my mouth with my hand. Had Tam

duped me into helping him arrange the American's murder? He'd obviously planned it with his friends—why else would the three of them have been waiting for him outside Givral?—but my contribution was crucial. I'd given him Buck's card and listened as he set the trap. I imagined him leading his friends inside the building and up to the second floor, where they'd have waited in the stairwell, just as I had done. Did Tam cry out, mid-act, to signal when the instant arrived to strike? The lurid scene played out in mind and would not go away, even when I closed my eyes.

"It is terrible, yes." Laurence put an arm around my shoulders and guided me out to the hall. By this time I was close to tears. One of the paratroopers handed me a handkerchief and I buried my face in the clean linen. *You'd have been worse than useless in the Resistance, going to pieces at the very moment when your comrades need you to be strong,* I berated myself. Striving to regain my composure, I went to the storeroom to fetch the key to the lavatory, doing my best to avert my eyes as I stepped around Buck's body. The key was not on its hook. Could they all be hiding in there? The bathroom was awfully small. To fit four people into a space that size, you'd have to cram them in like sardines. Given the heat, they'd have been suffocating after five minutes in that windowless room. No, it was more likely that Tam was alone. I shared my suspicions with Laurence, who conveyed then to her pals.

"*En avant,*" she said in a loud whisper. Forward. The airmen held their flashlights aloft as we inched along the corridor, prepared to use them as bludgeons at the first sign of trouble. When we reached the lavatory, I went to knock on the door, but was instructed to stay where I was and call to him from a safe distance.

"Tam, it's me, Cara." Silence. I looked to my companions, who indicated that I should keep talking. "Are you okay? It's safe to come out."

The lock clicked as he turned the knob. "Cara!" He emerged into the glare of the paratroopers' flashlights and in the instant before he shielded his eyes, I could see he'd been sick. Beads of perspiration trickled down his face and the stench of vomit wafted out through the open door. He was no better equipped for violence than I was.

A paratrooper stepped between us. *"Tu es seul là-bas?"* he demanded. Are you alone in there?

*"Oui, bien sûr."* Yes, of course.

*"Éloigne-toi de la porte."* Come away from the door. Shakily, Tam complied. With a quick motion, the airman kicked it open, revealing an empty room. Meanwhile, his colleague grabbed Tam roughly by the arm and began to interrogate him while Laurence stood by impassive.

*"Où sont-ils allés, les autres garçons?"* Where are the other boys?

*"Je—je—je ne sais pas,"* he stammered. I don't know.

*Vous avez attiré l'Américain au bureau pour le tuer, n'est-ce pas?"* You lured the American to the office in order to kill him, didn't you?"

Tam looked at the floor.

*"Réponds à la question!"* shouted the airman, tightening his grip.

*"Oui."*

*"Salaud!"* The first paratrooper slapped Tam across the face. I couldn't watch them hurt him, no matter what he'd done.

*"Permettez-moi?"* Without waiting for permission, I drew him away. "Now tell me what happened. I want to know the truth this time."

Tam took a deep breath and exhaled slowly. "They called me *kẻ phản bội*, a traitor of my own people."

"You're speaking of your friends?"

"The Việt Minh aren't my friends," he spat.

"Shhh." Nervously, I looked toward the others, but the three were conferring among themselves and paid us no heed. "Then why did you do it?"

"Do I need to spell it out for you? They threatened my mother. I couldn't run away and leave her to face the music."

Movie Western dialogue. Who said it and in which movie? He was resorting to his favorite game to distract me, but from what? Understanding dawned: the Việt Minh were the ones who showed up earlier at Lily's shop, not the police. They knew how to reach Tam in Gray's room. "You made them a deal, didn't you?" I said. "You offered up Buck in her place."

"What else could I do?"

*When evil strikes, you bow to circumstance.*

Laurence detached herself from her comrades and came over to join us. "*Tu peux y aller.*" You can go. We both stared at her in surprise. "*Aucun de nous ne veut être pris dans ce pétrin,*" she said with a shrug. "*Laissons les autres Américains s'en occuper.*" None of us wants to get caught up in this mess. Let the other Americans deal with it.

Tam turned on his heel and headed for the stairs without so much as a word goodbye. I considered calling after him—*Tam, come back*—but I knew his mind was set. He'd passed through an initiation rite and the Việt Minh owned him now. I wondered how long he'd last. For my brother's sake, I would do what I could to improve his chances.

I asked Laurence for the key to my office. The surveillance reports were no longer on Buck's desk, but I found them in the file cabinet, in a folder marked "Insurgent Activity:

Saigon." The American was nothing if not organized; an adjacent file labeled "Walden, Cara" contained a full account of my afternoon's exploits, along with a carbon copy of my paycheck. I added the original, threw in the photos of Gray for good measure, and tossed the lot into the first trashcan we passed on the way back to the Continental.

# CHAPTER SIXTEEN

## Notre-Dame Cathedral, Saigon
## March 9, 1957

The church was practically empty in the early evening. Jakub and I chose a side pew, away from the small cluster of worshipers who knelt, whispering prayers, on the prie-dieu on either side of the altar. In the quiet of the sanctuary, the sound of holy water dripping from the fountain behind us, I told him everything.

"You went back to the office?" My husband spoke with barely suppressed fury. "After what happened to you yesterday afternoon, I'd have expected you to show more sense. What were you thinking?"

I was thinking that he'd have done exactly the same, although on second thought, who was I kidding? Jakub wouldn't have been so stupid as to give Tam the American's phone number and let him walk into a trap, even if it was a trap of his own devising. He'd have kept Tam from leaving the hotel, never mind his friends. Buck would still be alive and by now we'd have come up with a way to spirit both Tam and his mother out of Vietnam. Everything had gone wrong and it was my fault.

"What did you say?"

"Oh, sorry." I hadn't realized I'd spoken aloud.

He gave me a penetrating look. "Is that why you pretended to be asleep when I returned from the party? I assumed you were giving me the silent treatment for staying out so late." He had been rather the worse for wear. I'd only just finished sweeping up the broken china when I heard the elevator, but his shuffling progress down the hall gave me ample time to turn out the lights and hop into bed.

"I couldn't face you last night," I told him.

My husband appeared not to have heard me. "Where did I put it?" he muttered, patting his jacket pockets. "Did I leave it in the room?"

"We ought to get back. Gray will be expecting an explanation."

"Right. The explanation." He passed me a folded sheet of hotel stationery. "I found it under the door this morning," he apologized. "You were still asleep . . ."

In tiny handwriting, Tam had written me a note: *Cara, Please give this to your brother*. Attached was his autographed photograph of Alan Ladd as Shane.

"Do you know what I was thinking as I was watching you sleep?" said Jakub tenderly. "I want us to have a child, *najdroższa*."

# Acknowledgments

Historical mysteries are travel literature with a kick. You get to visit a different locale, maybe a place you know—your own city, a century ago—but you're seeing it fresh. Danger sharpens your senses. Familiar landmarks fall away, comfortable habits of mind no longer fit as your focus shifts to accommodate new details of your surroundings, details your guide has brought to your attention. Or maybe you're the sort to venture abroad, exploring a distant place and era. New vistas, new sensations: you want to experience it all and, to paraphrase Humphrey Bogart in *The Maltese Falcon*, you don't mind a reasonable amount of trouble.

I set off on this foreign adventure with some marvelous guides, seasoned travelers who went to Vietnam in the 1950s, the decade when *The Glass Forest* is set. Norman Lewis chronicled his journey through Southeast Asia during the waning years of the French colonial empire in *A Dragon Apparent* (1951). His was largely a tale of desultory conversations with besieged French administrators in remote outposts, heavy drinking among tribal peoples, death-defying drives through risky territory, all narrated with classic British understatement. Along the way he described an encounter with a French anthropologist who had "gone native" after living among the Khmer and witnessing their enslavement at the hands of French rubber planters—the inspiration for my character, Ta Philippe.

Graham Greene followed in Lewis's footsteps and I, in turn, have followed Greene, aided by Tim Doling's handy guide to historic Saigon, *Exploring Ho Chi Minh City* (2014). *The Glass Forest* pays tribute to *The Quiet American* (1955), my favorite of Greene's novels, while interposing the appealing, damaged Tam as the embodiment of Vietnam—a more potent symbol than Greene's childlike Phuong—and making the story hinge on his political awakening. Tam is nowhere near as devious as the *Time* magazine reporter and Vietnamese Communist agent who was the subject of Larry Berman's biography, *Perfect Spy: The Incredible Double Life of Pham Xuan An* (2007), but Berman's book showed me what was possible. And during a 2016 research trip to Ho Chi Minh City, my husband and I were given the room in the Continental Hotel where An hid out with his mother after the American evacuation.

I met the intrepid Laurence in Bernard Fall's eyewitness account of the French loss at Dien Bien Phu, *Street Without Joy* (1961). Brigitte Friang was a reporter covering the war when Fall knew her in Saigon; like him, she'd joined the Resistance fresh out of school, but her unit was betrayed to the Gestapo and Friang was tortured for a year before being deported to Ravensbrück, marking her indelibly. "Impeccably attired in black tulle evening gown," wrote Fall, "Brigitte Friang looked like any girl should look, except for her gray-blue eyes. No matter how gay the conversation, how relaxed the evening, Brigitte's eyes never seemed quite reconciled to smiling." Intrigued, I read Friang's memoir, *Regarde-toi qui meurs* (1997) [Look at yourself, dying], and found a place for her in my story.

Getting back to Bernard Fall, my discussion of Viet Minh activity in the Mekong Delta owes much to the investigative articles he published in foreign policy magazines (collected and republished in 1966 as *Viet-Nam Witness*). He was the first to reveal the pattern of "spectacular assassinations" in the South, beginning in 1957, which he regarded as an indication of the failure of America's counterinsurgency policy. Alongside the standard histories of Stanley Karnow, Fredrik Logevall, David Halberstam and Neil Sheehan, Kathryn Statler's *Replacing France: The Origins of American Intervention in Vietnam* (2007) provided a useful account of the American build-up in this early period.

I would like to thank Duong Van Thanh, Academic Director of the SIT Study Abroad program in Vietnam, for her warm welcome during our visit to Ho Chí Minh City. Thanh has her own story to tell about her childhood in Hanoi, and I hope she will find the time to write it down. Thanks also to the Reid Cinema Archives at Wesleyan University for granting me access to the William Hornbeck Collection. Hornbeck's shooting diary from the months he spent on location in Saigon as editor on the Joseph Mankiewicz production of *The Quiet American* furnished me with a structure for my book, while his letters to his wife were an incomparable source of day-to-day details about everything from black market currency exchange rates to the feeding habits of lizards in Saigon hotel rooms.

I am fortunate to have Lourdes Venard as my editor, Deirdre Wait as my cover designer, and Eddie Vincent for layout and ebook conversion. Owing to their high standards, the Cara Walden mysteries have garnered notice in national review outlets. Tim Lang, the genius behind Passport Press, has been my fellow adventurer for forty years and the road still beckons. *En avant!*

# About the Author

L isa Lieberman writes the Cara Walden series of historical mysteries based on old movies and featuring blacklisted Hollywood people on the lam in dangerous international locales. Trained as a modern European cultural and intellectual historian, she has written extensively on postwar Europe. Lieberman has published essays, translations, and short stories in Noir City, Gettysburg Review, Raritan, Michigan Quarterly, Mystery Scene and various anthologies, and is the founder of the classic movie blog Deathless Prose. After dragging their three children all over Europe while they were growing up, Lisa and her husband are happily settled in Amherst, Massachusetts with their Scottish Terrier, Hume.

CPSIA information can be obtained
at www.ICGtesting.com
Printed in the USA
FFHW020744291119
56124645-62236FF